WYCLIFFE
AND DEATH IN STANLEY STREET

The murder of a prostitute in the dubious cul-de-sac of a West Country port is just another routine sex crime to Inspector Gill. However, when Superintendent Wycliffe investigates the girl's past, he finds that Lily Painter had several 'O' and 'A' levels to her name, and liked Beethoven—not the usual sort of prostitute at all. He digs deeper, and finds plenty of surprises, starting with her parents, and a shadowy connection with property speculators and drug smugglers. A second murder and a dangerous arson attack take place before Wycliffe is able to discover the solution to the complex puzzle.

WYCLIFFE
AND DEATH IN STANLEY STREET

WYCLIFFE
And Death In
Stanley Street

by
W. J. Burley

Magna Large Print Books
Long Preston, North Yorkshire,
England.

British Library Cataloguing in Publication Data.

Burley, W. J.
    Wycliffe and death in Stanley Street.

A catalogue record for this book is
available from the British Library

ISBN 0-7505-1143-5

First published in Great Britain by Victor Gollancz Ltd., 1974

Copyright © 1974 by W. J. Burley

Cover illustration by arrangement with H.T.V.

Published in Large Print 1997 by arrangement with Victor
Gollancz

Magna Large Print is an imprint of
Library Magna Books Ltd.
Printed and bound in Great Britain by
T.J. International Ltd., Cornwall, PL28 8RW.

CHAPTER ONE

Stanley Street is a cul-de-sac, blocked at the far end by iron railings which separate it from the railway embankment. The houses are cheap because of the trains but they are convenient for the shops. Prince's Street, the main thoroughfare between the docks and the city centre, is only a block away and the muffled roar of its traffic fills the gaps between the trains so that there is little risk of silence except at odd times in the small hours and on Sunday mornings.

Most of the shops in Prince's Street are real shops, not department stores or supermarkets, and most of them spill over on to the pavements. There are bakers who bake crusty bread, butchers who sell undyed meat (not in plastic bags), grocers, greengrocers, delicatessens, wine shops, tobacconists, stationers and ironmongers. And there is at least one pub every two hundred yards.

There are twenty-two houses in Stanley

Street, most of them are dilapidated, but three or four have been converted into flats: two flats to each house with a shared front door. The flats are occupied by single girls who spend most of their days in bed and start work after the shops in Prince's Street have closed. A base in Stanley Street is convenient for pick-ups who dislike having to walk far. Most nights there are plenty of pick-ups: seamen from the docks, a few students sampling life in the raw and several middle-aged husbands and fathers from the suburbs. Each girl has her beat which includes at least one pub.

'Hullo, darling!'

Brenda was standing in the side entrance to a newsagent's. The barman at The Joiners had warned her off because the cops were taking an interest in the place. It was a nuisance but it would pass, it always did. The police were not interested in her, they were after pushers and somebody had tipped them off about The Joiners. Good luck to them, she didn't like pushers either but she couldn't afford to stick her neck out.

'Hullo, darling, want to come home?'

It was drizzling rain, not many people about, just cars and the occasional lorry swishing through. Four days to Christmas and business was always bad at holiday time, especially Christmas. She was on the point of turning it in for the night, she was cold and the damp seemed to penetrate right through her. She walked a little way down the pavement to stand under the shelter of the railway bridge.

'Hullo, darling.'

A little fellow, his mackintosh buttoned up to the neck; in his fifties or older. He stopped to look at her with hungry, timorous eyes.

'I'll give you a nice time. Number 9 Stanley Street, just round the corner. Go in and right up the stairs.'

The patter came automatically then she turned and walked off, leaving him standing. She didn't care a damn whether he followed her or not, she'd had enough. She turned the corner into Wellington Road, fifty yards along then another corner into Stanley Street. The houses were on one side only, facing the wall of a wholesale grocery warehouse. Most of the houses retained their little pocket-handkerchief gardens with hedges of jaded privet. The door of number nine was unlocked and there was a light in the hall. Another girl,

Lily Painter, occupied the ground floor flat. The door of her front room was shut which meant that she was at home and engaged with a client. Probably 'Daddy', Brenda thought vaguely, it was his night.

She called, 'It's me, Lily,' and went on up the stairs.

They got on well together. Lily was twenty-six, five years younger. She was vivacious, pretty too, with a figure which took years off the old men and she was so popular that her clients came by appointment. Brenda felt no jealousy, you had to be realistic and it was a question of supply and demand. All the same, she sometimes wondered.

At the top of the stairs, two rooms with a tiny kitchen and an even tinier bathroom and loo. One of the rooms was her bedroom, the other a sitting-room which she kept private; no client was ever admitted. To make sure, it was always locked. She hung her wet mackintosh on a hanger and put it to drip over the bath. In the bedroom she turned up the gas fire, kicked off her shoes and unzipped her dress. For a moment she stood, in briefs and brassière, looking at herself in the dressing-table mirror. She was painfully thin, her ribs showed under her small breasts; her skin was white, bleached looking. She knew that most of her customers were disappointed when they saw her naked. She was thirty-two and she had no need of a clairvoyant to tell her that it would not be long before she began to look haggard. Her mother had lost what looks she ever had while she was in her thirties. Brenda put on her red dressing-gown of brushed nylon. She liked red, it seemed to go with her jet black hair and it made her thin, pale face look interesting.

In the kitchen she took a bottle of brandy from a cupboard and poured herself a tot. She drank it off and it warmed her, she felt better. She had forgotten about the man until she heard his slow footsteps on the stairs. She met him on the landing and took his wet coat. He came into the bedroom in a daze. She noticed that he was lame, trailing his left foot.

'I'll take it now, love—the money.'

He fumbled in his wallet and produced a couple of notes; she smiled and slipped them into a drawer of the bedside table.

'Aren't you going to take your clothes off?'

She lay on top of the bed and opened her dressing-gown. He tried to kiss her but she told him not to, which put him off.

'I'm sorry.'

'No need to apologise, dear, but we got to be careful else we'd catch everything that was going.'

'Yes, of course, I didn't think.'

She felt sorry for this sad little man and tried to help him. 'You married?'

'Sort of.'

It was soon over.

'The bathroom is at the top of the stairs.'

He went off, carrying his jacket and trousers. A few minutes later he put his head round the door, 'Thank you.' She helped him on with his wet coat and heard him clip-clop down the stairs, making heavy weather of it with his game leg.

A few minutes in the bathroom. Half past nine, too early to go to bed. She unlocked the door of her sitting-room. A cosy little room, suburban, with a three piece suite, a fitted carpet, television and a picture of elephants trumpeting through African dust over the mantelpiece. She switched on the fire and the telly. No cigarettes. She went to the top of the stairs to see if Lily was still engaged. Daddy must have left for Lily's door was slightly ajar; she would be tidying up. A three-and-a-half litre Rover or a Mercedes parked two or three streets away and in a few minutes Daddy would be back in his detached residence in Edgington or Farley and Mrs Daddy would say that he looked tired and offer him dry sherry.

She flip-flopped downstairs in her slippers and as she reached the hall the telephone rang. '70862. This is Bren—OK. See you next week then. Don't do anything I wouldn't.'

One of her few regulars calling off for the week.

She dropped the receiver back on its rest and went into Lily's sitting-room. It was very different from hers, more elegant and part of the business. There was a glass fronted cabinet with drinks for the clients, before, after or in between. Your feet sank into coffee coloured pile and there were erotic pictures on the wall: a series depicting sculptural reliefs from the temple of Khajuraho. Unassailable as works of art but effective as a mild stimulant for the jaded client without the implied insult of merely dirty pictures.

To Brenda's surprise the room was only lit by light coming through the open door of the bedroom.

'Lily, are you there?' For some reason she was nervous and her voice cracked.

Apart from being attractive Lily was educated and this went down well with a certain type of client. Intelligent conversation added a redeeming gloss to what might otherwise appear a sordid encounter. Of course, they paid for it.

'Lily?'

From the bedroom a door opened into a well-appointed bathroom all in shades of pink. Lily's bed was pink too and frilly, surrounded by wall mirrors. Lily was lying on the bed, on her back, her feet just touching the carpet, and she was naked, her small, girlish breasts wide apart. She was dead, her face contorted and frightful. Her reflection in the wall mirrors added another dimension in the grotesque.

Brenda did not scream or panic but she felt a sudden constriction in her stomach which made her want to vomit. She fought it down.

999—She dialled.

'Which service do you require?'

'Police.'

A click. 'Police.'

She began incoherently.

'Please state your name, where you are speaking from and the number of your telephone.'

She managed it.

'Have you called a doctor?'

'She's dead! I keep telling you.'

'All the same... Please wait where you are and touch nothing. One of our cars will be with you in a few minutes.'

They seemed to take it as though it were an everyday event—so bloody calm. But for her it was Lily, one of the few people she could call a friend. For three years they had lived in the same house.

She opened the front door and stood on the step, she could not bear it inside. It was raining hard now. She heard the siren of a police car coming down Prince's Street. It turned into Wellington Road and the tyres screeched on the streaming tarmac as it made a second sharp turn into Stanley Street. The siren wailed to silence and two young coppers got out.

'Where is she, love?'

One of them went in to see while the other stayed with her. He was gentle. 'Brenda, isn't it?' She remembered him.

He was fair haired and red faced, a regular country boy. He had booked her once for too blatantly soliciting, she had been going through a bad patch. 'Is there somewhere we can talk?'

The other came out of Lily's flat, grim faced, nodded to his mate and went out to the car. 'I'll report back.'

Upstairs in the kitchen, a policeman's cap on the plastic-topped table, his notebook open beside it. She could hear voices downstairs, probably the doctor had arrived.

'Lily Painter,' the young man wrote in his book. 'Any relatives that you know of?'

'She never mentioned anybody. She told me once that her parents were both dead.' It was true, although they were friendly Lily said very little about herself or her family.

'You found her?'

'I went down to cadge a cigarette.'

'And just found her lying there—is that it?' He was looking at her with earnest blue eyes, trying to do his job without upsetting her.

Suddenly her heart seemed to stop. 'It must have been him!'

'Who, love?'

'The man who killed her—Daddy she calls him, he's one of her regulars and tonight was his night.'

'Who is he?'

She looked at him blankly. 'I've no idea, but it must have been him mustn't it? I mean, he must have been with her when I came in.' She shivered at the thought.

'Have you ever seen him?'

'Not to say seen him, just glimpsed him, coming in or going out.'

'Can you describe him?'

'Not really, he's oldish.'

'How old?'

She shrugged. 'Fifty? I don't know, do I? I only set eyes on him two or three times and that was in the hall where there isn't much light. Besides, they don't like being stared at.'

Another siren, getting nearer.

'The Brass.'

'He's been coming regular for a long time, she used to laugh about him—'

'Try to remember.'

She frowned. 'He was not very tall—on the small side. I think he was dark but I'm not sure. Perhaps he was grey—oh! and he wore a grey, herring-bone tweed overcoat, I remember that.'

'No hat?'

'No.'

'A bit posh?'

'I suppose he was—he would need to be to go to Lily.'

'Did you ever speak to him?'

She shook her head.

'Never mind, make yourself a cup of tea, love, you'll have visitors in a minute.'

She could hear them downstairs, and yet another siren. The telephone rang in the hall.

'Don't bother, they'll answer it.'

Detective Chief Inspector Gill was very tall, very thin, he stooped as a matter of habit. A large face with rubbery features and a permanent five-o'clock shadow. She had had customers like him, they left you sore inside and bruised out. He had a girl with him, a female dick in a turtle-necked sweater and a mini-skirt. Brenda had had dealings with her sort, too. They were supposed to comfort you and catch you off balance at the same time.

The young constable handed his note-book to the big man who glanced at it, snapped it shut and tucked it into the constable's tunic pocket.

'Give it to Sergeant Scales downstairs and tell him to have the description put out. As for you, lad, back on watch!' His eyes came round to Brenda. 'What's this then? Making tea? Sue can do that, it's one of her few talents. Where are we?' He was opening doors off the landing. 'This'll do, in here.'

She followed him into her sitting-room where the gas fire seemed welcoming and the television was on showing the inevitable football match.

'Sit down.' He stood over the television set, watching. 'Christ! You'd think some of 'em had two left feet and creeping bloody paralysis.' He switched the set off and turned to her. 'Not working tonight?'

She did not answer and he grinned. He sat in the easy chair opposite her and lit a long, black cheroot. 'Now tell uncle all about it.'

She did and he questioned her minutely.

'This chap she called Daddy; what did she tell you about him?'

'Nothing much, just that he was kinky and she used to laugh at him. A lot of the old ones have kinky tricks.'

'What sort of tricks did he have?'

'He likes doing himself up in leather straps and he brings pictures.'

'Pictures?'

'To look at. Some of them are really past it.'

'Is that all?'

She shrugged. 'All she told me.'

From time to time trains passed at the end of the road, the house shook and the windows rattled.

'Now, what about this description, you can do better than that.'

The policewoman brought in tea but Brenda's went cold before she could drink it.

'You haven't got a ponce have you?'

'No.'

'Did she?'

A faint smile. 'I can't see any man getting money out of Lily.'

He clicked his tongue. 'Greedy, both of you. You need somebody to look after you in this game.' He flicked ash into the gas fire. 'No maid?'

'No.'

'You two in the house alone?'

'Yes.'

'Bloody asking for it.' He stood up and glanced round the little room. 'Nice if you can keep it. Anyway, I'm off. You can start telling Sue all about it.'

'But I've told you.'

He grinned, his greasy rubbery grin which showed all his teeth. 'You haven't started to tell anything yet, girlie.' At the door her turned, 'And Sue, get her to give you a description of that chap she had with her—'

'He doesn't know anything.'

'Let him tell it.' He went out, closing the door.

'His bark is worse than his bite, don't let it get you down.'

She felt constrained to put on a front. 'His sort don't worry me, I've seen too many.'

The WPC was a homely sort of girl after all. She was plump and not bad looking. She sat in the chair her boss had vacated.

'You didn't get your tea, I'll make you another pot.'

'No, I will, I'd feel better doing something.'

'Let's do it together.'

Both in the kitchen. Something like it was with Lily. Often they would muck in together and usually, for some reason, it was in Brenda's kitchen. 'More homely than my place,' Lily used to say.

'You were fond of her?'

'In a way.'

'Tough.'

It wasn't long before they were chatting like any two young women. Relaxed. They boiled a couple of eggs and ate them seated at the kitchen table. 'A funny sort of job, yours,' Brenda said, thoughtfully.

The girl looked at her and laughed. 'You should talk!'

What was the difference between them? Five or six years and four or five 'O' levels? More than that. Something fundamental.

'Now about this chap you were with...'

At one o'clock the policewoman said, 'I'd get some sleep if I were you, the circus will start again tomorrow.'

She yawned. 'I think I'll give it a try.'

'I can stay the night if you like?'

'No thanks, I'll be OK.'

'Have you got any tablets to make you sleep?'

Downstairs they were still at work. Lily's flat seemed to be full of men and there were cables everywhere for camera lights. Sergeant Smith, the squad's photographer, cursed steadily. 'Not room to stand sideways in this bloody place, you need a sodding sky-hook.' But in the end the girl's body had been photographed from every possible angle and removed for the autopsy. Then came photographs of the rooms and after that Sergeant Scales, the finger-print expert, moved in. He needed Smith's help to photograph prints which were accessible to the camera, those which were not had to be 'taken off' on tape and photographed later. Finally, a meticulous search undertaken by Scales and an assistant in which they all but took the flat apart.

But there was nothing surprising in what they found, more in what they did not find. No letters, not a single photograph, no papers, nothing which helped to put her in the context of a family, almost nothing to relate her to any life outside the flat. There was an engagement book in which appointments were recorded by initials, sometimes only a single letter. The entry for that evening was JH.

Stanley Street had not seen such activity since the war when all the houses on the opposite side of the street had been destroyed. Police cars and motor cycles were coming and going continuously and detectives went from house to house asking questions and collecting varied and unhelpful answers.

'Well, it's no surprise really, is it? I mean, if you go on like that what can you expect?'

'The men! Beastly, I call it. No, I haven't seen anybody tonight; I mean, I don't take that much notice and it was dark anyway. It's when they come in the afternoon, as bold as brass...'

'I thought it was illegal...'

'I keep to myself, what other people do...'

A lot of it got written down.

At two o'clock in the morning CID headquarters were still a blaze of light and Chief Superintendent Wycliffe was at his desk. Typewriters were clacking and telephones ringing all over the place. Organized chaos. Chief Inspector Gill was lolling in a swivel chair opposite his chief. The two men could hardly have been less alike. Wycliffe, barely regulation height, looking more like a lean and kindly monk than a policeman; Gill, six feet four in his socks, a face like a rubber mould, extroverted and often coarse.

'We shall have to keep tags on all the whores in town, these cases are never one-off.'

Wycliffe did not answer, he was scraping out the bowl of his pipe into an ash-tray. At the beginning of a case he liked to avoid discussion but thinking aloud seemed to be essential to Gill's mental processes. He tried again.

'Who's doing the PM?'

'Franks, he promised to look in on his way home.'

A messenger came in with a sheaf of photographs of the girl and Wycliffe picked through them impatiently. 'I asked for something we could give the newspapers.'

'Sergeant Smith is working on it, sir. He says it will take him another hour.'

Gill chucked. 'What did he really say?'

'Sir?'

Smith was a morose dyspeptic who declared most things he was asked to do to be impossible but did them just the same.

Wycliffe asked the messenger, 'Will three o'clock be time enough?'

'For the city edition of *The News*, yes, sir.'

Gill was curious. 'You seem to think

there's going to be some trouble over indentification.'

Wycliffe shrugged. 'I shall be surprised if there isn't. A girl on the game who makes a point of having no papers about her.'

Gill blew out a cloud of blue-grey smoke. 'I can't see that it matters, except technically; her killer didn't care a damn who she was.'

'We don't know that.'

'I'd take a bet.'

Wycliffe lit his pipe, puffing hard to get it going. 'Lily Painter—it sounds a bit phoney, don't you think?'

'I don't see why, there must be scores of Painters in the phone book and plenty of girls are called Lily, even in these days.'

'Maybe you're right.' But Wycliffe was not convinced. Lily Painter—the painter of lilies, gilder of lilies? Too fanciful for Gill, perhaps too fanciful for common sense.

Elsewhere in the building a circular was being prepared for tailors and outfitters about herring-bone tweed overcoats. A questionnaire was being drafted in preparation for a more exhaustive house-to-house. It asked for information about cars parked nearby and for news of anyone out and about in the area at the time of the crime. Detectives were going through the Voters' lists for initials which corresponded with those in Lily's engagement book. Lily, herself, was not on the Voters' lists.

A few respected citizens were going to feel a cold draught for a day or two and certain abused wives might get a fresh hold on their husbands.

Wycliffe was shuffling through Smith's photographs of the dead girl's body and of the room. He picked up one and passed it to Gill.

'What do you make of the damage to her neck? It looks as though the skin was broken just below the larynx.'

'It was.'

'What did he use?'

'His hands, the marks of his fingers are clear on the back of her neck. The injury in front was caused by a clasp or brooch. She was wearing a high-necked dress with a stand-up collar held together in front by this brooch. His thumbs must have been on the brooch, there's blood on the inside of the dress collar—not much, but enough.'

Wycliffe looked at Gill in surprise. 'So she was dressed when she was strangled?'

'It certainly looks like it.'

'But naked when she was found; so, presumably, the strangler stripped her body after death. Why would he do that?'

Gill was finding himself on the defensive without quite knowing how he got there. 'Because he was kinky, I suppose.'

Both men knew the usual pattern of sex crimes only too well.

'Where were her clothes?'

Gill got up and shuffled through the preliminary reports on Wycliffe's desk. 'There you are: a Paisley patterned dress, a nylon slip, brassière, briefs and tights, all lying on a sort of upholstered chest at the bottom of the bed.'

'Thrown or placed there, would you say?'

Gill reflected. 'Placed.'

'Just as a reasonably careful woman might do if she undressed herself?'

'I suppose so, but I don't see—'

Wycliffe was studying another of Smith's photographs. 'Look at this one. It shows the body on the bed and, as far as I can see, there's been very little disturbance, the bedding is scarcely rumpled.'

'That's right, it wasn't.' Gill scattered ash on the carpet. 'I take your point, we've got a very careful, methodical killer but I don't see where it gets us. What does it matter?'

Wycliffe scooped the photographs into a pile. 'All I'm saying is that it's an unusual sex crime.'

'A kink who lingered over his work.'

'Perhaps, but isn't it equally possible that he was trying to make his crime look like a sex killing?'

Gill stubbed out the butt of his cheroot. 'I suppose you've got a point there. We shall soon know. If he runs true to form there'll be another killing before long.'

'You sent the clothing to Forensic?'

'Of course.'

'And the brooch?'

'That's gone too. Scales checked it for prints but there was no surface to take them.'

'Handbag?'

'She had a handbag—tissues, compact, lipstick, a few pounds in cash, no keys.'

'You found no keys at all?'

Gill shook his head. 'No, it's odd. The tart upstairs says she had a key-ring with several keys on it and a charm.'

At half past two Dr Franks, the pathologist, arrived. As bouncy as ever, he looked as though he had just come from his morning shower, all talcum and aftershave. He had worked with Wycliffe so often that he regarded himself as one of the team.

'Not much for you, gentlemen. She was strangled, of course.'

'Big deal!' from Gill.

'Strangled with bare hands but the pressure below the larynx was applied through a brooch or something of that sort. The killer must have been facing her. I gather she was wearing a high-necked dress with a brooch that would fit the facts, his thumbs must have been on that.'

'Any sign of a struggle?'

'No other marks on the body except for two bruises inside the thighs, and they were not recent.'

'What about intercourse before or after death?'

The chubby doctor shook his head. 'No evidence but that doesn't mean a great deal.'

'She was on the pill,' Gill said.

'Even so, most of these girls want another kind of protection with strangers.'

'Perhaps he wasn't a stranger.'

'In my view that's more than likely,' Wycliffe said.

Franks looked puzzled and Gill explained. 'The chief thinks it might not be the usual thing—not a sex crime.'

Franks shrugged. 'I can't see that it makes any difference at this stage.'

'It makes a great deal of difference. In the one case, we are looking for someone who is pathologically disturbed, who might kill any available woman; in the other, we are after a man who had, what seemed to him, a good reason to kill this particular girl.' Wycliffe made a gesture of impatience and changed the subject. 'What about the time of death?'

'As near as I can put it between half past eight and nine.'

Wycliffe referred to his notes. 'The girl from the top flat arrived back about a quarter to nine when she says the door into the dead girl's room was closed. It was nine-thirty-five when she rang 999 but before that she had stopped to answer the telephone in the hall. The door was then a little open. If she is right the killer probably left between eight-forty-five and nine-thirty.'

'Which fits,' Franks said.

Wycliffe stood up. 'I'm for bed.'

He drove home through deserted streets.

He had been in the city for a month. In a political deal Area Police Headquarters had been transferred there and CID had followed. He wasn't sorry, the sprawling, bustling port pleased him better than the rather inward looking cathedral city from which he had come. On the debit side he had exchanged offices in a Queen Anne crescent for one floor in a wing of the new Area HQ. On the credit side he had bought a substantial granite-built house in half an acre of ground overlooking the estuary, and an endless panorama of ships steamed through the narrows at the bottom of his garden. For weeks Helen had been organizing workmen who would, one day, expect to be paid. He had never known her so content; so much she had scarcely noticed her fortieth birthday.

It troubled his socialist conscience sometimes. He felt that he had betrayed some thing, perhaps himself. Charlie Wycliffe, copper and Helen Wills, typist, buying beauty and privacy in this overcrowded island.

Bah! He worked hard.

Anyway it was a good feeling as he turned off the road down a gravelled track which led only to his own property. A white, five-barred gate. WATCH HOUSE in white letters on a varnished plaque. Away to his right he could look down on the water gleaming dimly in the near-darkness. Navigation lights, some steady, some winking. It seemed a long way from prostitutes and sex crimes and police reports; but away to the north the lights of the city still flared in the night sky.

CHAPTER TWO

Stanley Street looked drab in the light of a grey morning. Wycliffe drove slowly down it and stopped at number nine. Opposite, one of the steel shutters of the grocery warehouse had been raised and a van had backed in to load with tinned soups, cornflakes and baked beans (3p off). No sign of the excitement of the previous night. 9 Stanley Street was now 'on file', its essence distilled into a few sheets of typescript, three or four scale drawings and a score of photographs. But Wycliffe was seeing it for the first time. There was no need for him to see it now. His job was to delegate and to co-ordinate, sitting in his nice new office but, as more than one of his subordinates had remarked, 'There's no show without Punch'.

The house was better cared for than most of the houses, the woodwork was fresh with apple-green paint, otherwise it was like the rest, like thousands built before the first war. A porch over the front door was supported on wooden pillars and next to the front door there was a big bay-window. The window of number nine was curtained with fine net.

Wycliffe's ring was answered by a constable who had been left on watch, though what he was supposed to watch nobody had told him.

'Busy?'

'No, sir, not exactly.'

'No, you wouldn't be, my boy, not in here, all the villains are out there.'

The constable had heard stories, there was a veritable folk-lore surrounding the superintendent, now he had a story of his own.

'Is she up yet?' Wycliffe jerked his thumb in the direction of the stairs.

'I haven't heard her moving about yet, sir.'

'All right, off you go.'

Wycliffe broke the seal on the door leading into the dead girl's flat. The room was almost in darkness; heavy velvet curtains inside the net, screened the window. He whisked them back and let in the cold steely light. The morning after. Stale cigarette smoke mixed with the stink of flash-bulbs and faint, clinging perfume. Muddy footmarks on the carpet and tobacco ash left by his policemen, none of them house trained. He heard the front door slam behind the constable and his spirits rose. Apart from the girl upstairs he had the place to himself.

He looked at the pictures on the walls, poked about in the drinks cupboard where there were several bottles unopened: whisky, rum, gin, brandy and several sherries, even a Madeira. All tastes catered for, no expense spared. The glasses hadn't come out of a chain store either. Evidently she had a discerning clientèle. Odd that she chose to do it in a shabby back street. Odd, until you remembered that her customers could feel anonymous here, it was neutral ground. In any case a well-off neighbourhood wouldn't have stood for her line of business.

Not much furniture. The room was on the small side but what there was had style; a long settee upholstered in creamy-white leather and armchairs to match, a couple of low tables on castors and a bench with a stereo record player and a record rack underneath. There was a record on the turntable—Beethoven's Sonata in F for violin and piano. Wycliffe set it going.

Cheerful, almost frivolous. Her taste or her customer's? Wycliffe let it play while he went into the bedroom.

Coffee and cream in the reception, pink in the bedroom. The other room had not looked like a brothel, this did. The carpet was pink, so were the bedclothes, all of them. The bed took up most of the space but there was a small dressing-table and a built-in wardrobe in white. Pink and white. It reminded Wycliffe of sugar covered biscuits he had been expected to like as a child and it made him feel slightly sick as they had done. Everything was confusingly duplicated in the wall mirrors. There were two doors with mirror panels, one into the pink bathroom and the other into a white, thank God, kitchen.

He rooted about in the drawers of the dressing-table. Cosmetics and toilet articles, a few bits of jewellery in a little teakwood box. The wardrobe was small and held a trouser suit, three rather severe looking woollen dresses and a varied collection of housecoats-cum-dressing-gowns. There were trays holding tights and brassières and a rack with three pairs of shoes. There were slippers (pink) on the floor.

'Who are you?'

He had not heard her until she spoke because of the music. She stood in the doorway of the bedroom, thin, pale, her black hair hanging lank and straight to her shoulders. She wore a red dressing-gown of brushed nylon which probably made her look paler than she was.

Wycliffe introduced himself. 'Are you Brenda?'

'I heard the music.'

'She didn't really live here, did she?'

'I don't know what you mean.'

'Any coffee upstairs?'

'If you like.'

He followed her up the stairs. In the kitchen she filled an electric kettle and switched it on.

'It's only instant.'

'Do you mind if I look round?'

'Help yourself.' Resigned.

He looked into the sitting-room with its picture of stampeding elephants over the fireplace. The mantelshelf was crowded with little china and glass animals and in one corner there was a glass-fronted cabinet with a lot more. He looked into the bedroom which was like a demonstration room in a chain-store showroom, all plastic and veneer, but he liked it better than the one downstairs.

'Your coffee's made.'

The kitchen window looked out over a concrete yard with the backs of Prince's Street beyond; but she had fitted red and white checked curtains which made the outlook seem almost gay.

'I said that she didn't *live* in that flat downstairs. You live here, anybody can see that.'

'It's true she was away a lot. Most nights she didn't sleep there and she was hardly ever there in the afternoons or all day on Sundays.'

'Where did she spend the rest of her time?'

Brenda shrugged. 'She never gave much away and I've found it best not to ask questions. Sugar?'

'No thanks.' He stirred his coffee. 'We didn't find any keys.'

She frowned. 'No, they told me. She had a key-ring with three or four keys on it including one to the front door downstairs.'

'You'd better get the lock changed.'

Wycliffe had a copy of the photograph which had appeared in the paper. Sergeant

Smith had done him proud. Nobody would have suspected that the photograph had been taken after death, least of all after death by strangulation.

'What do you think of this?' He put the photograph on the table among the coffee cups.

'Where did you get that? I've never seen a photo of her before.'

'Is it like her?'

'Of course it's like her, it *is* her.' She seemed to hesitate.

'Well?'

'It's just that she looks different, sort of blank.'

'Last night you told Mr Gill that she was educated. What did you mean?'

'Well, she had lots of "O" levels and "A" levels, that sort of thing.' She brought out a packet of cigarettes from the pocket of her dressing-gown and offered it to Wycliffe. 'Cigarette?'

'No thanks—pipe.' He got out his pouch and started to fill it. 'Did she go to school here in the city?'

'I suppose so, she never mentioned anywhere else.' Brenda was not bright and she seemed to be almost totally lacking in curiosity.

41

'You think she was a local girl?'

'Oh, yes, I think so.' She lit a cigarette, inhaled and coughed.

'Why?'

Brenda looked vague. She got up to brush the fragments of Wycliffe's tobacco into an ashtray. The kitchen, like the rest of the flat, was spotless.

'When did you first meet her?'

The smooth, sallow skin of her brow wrinkled. 'Two—three years ago. She had a beat then, like me. She said she was learning the job and asked me if I would share a house with her. She told me she was going to rent this place in Stanley Street.'

'You paid her rent for this flat?'

'Yes.'

'Did she sting you?'

The tired, dark eyes widened. 'Not really. It's a job to get a place where the landlord or the neighbours don't complain. I was lucky.'

She was thirty-one or two and she looked older. An interesting face, thin but not sharp, a good, straight nose and rather fine, dark eyes. She could have been sitting across the breakfast table from her husband. Why wasn't she? Was it fear? Or

42

an odd sort of courage? She wasn't happy but she was not alone in that.

'What sort of a girl was Lily?'

Again the puzzled frown. The question was too much for her but she made the effort. 'She was queer. You never knew with her. She would say things.'

Wycliffe was smoking peaceably. 'What things?'

'Half the time I didn't know what she was getting at. She used to look at me and say things like, "You don't hate them, do you, Bren?" Another time it would be, "You're a bloody fool. You let them screw you but I screw them—and bloody how."' She looked at Wycliffe almost shyly as though she hoped that he might explain.

'Anything else?'

'She used to ask me about my family, especially about my father, whether he was a bastard and all that.'

'Was he?'

She pursed her lips. 'I've never really thought about it. I mean, you don't, do you?'

'Did she ever tell you about her father or her family?'

'Never.'

They sat in silence for a while and when

she got up she took the dishes to the sink and started washing them. 'I suppose I shall have to find somewhere else.'

'I shouldn't be in a hurry, this is going to take some sorting out.'

She turned to him with a faint smile, the first he had seen on her pale solemn face. 'You're a funny sort of cop.'

Bellings, his immediate superior, would have said 'Amen' to that.

Wycliffe drove back to his headquarters through heavy traffic in the mid-morning rush. He was more than ever convinced that Lily Painter of 9 Stanley Street had had another address, another identity. It was important to know about her life away from Stanley Street and this must be his first priority.

On the way down the corridor to his office he stopped at Administration.

'Who's free?'

The constable in charge of work schedules was a young man with aspirations and the sense to see that a modern police force runs on paper. He consulted his records. 'DCs Dixon, Fowler, and Shaw, sir.'

'Send Dixon and Fowler to my office. Enquiries concerning the murdered girl.'

Wycliffe had not yet settled down in his

new office, he doubted if he ever would. The wood panelling 'it's real, not vinyl or laminate', the sectional bookcases with law books and police reports he would never open, one of those great square desks which looked as though it had been spawned in congress between a teak tree and a plastics factory and the horrid, ornamented grille spewing out tepid, deoxygenated air with controls offering a choice between suffocation and frost bite.

Another innovation was a young woman in an office next to his, WPC Saxton. She was blonde with aristocratic features and she looked as though she had just emerged from the proverbial bandbox. She regarded him, so he claimed, with a mixture of tolerance and contempt which made him uncomfortable. She was there to look after him and she was conscientious.

On his desk, among the reports, there was an abstract of the Voters' lists giving the names of certain men whose initials matched those in Lily's engagement book. The searchers had confined their attention to areas of the city where better-off people lived, for the others would not have been able to afford Lily. There had been four entries in her diary with two initials and two with only a single letter to identify the client. Wycliffe's men had concentrated on those with two initials but, even so, the list ran to more than two hundred names. Now it was a question of going to work diplomatically, and patiently trying to eliminate the non-starters. A dozen men would be kept busy but it had to be done. Delicate too. Touch one tender spot and the whole thing would blow up in his face.

Detective Constable Dixon arrived, he was a new member of the squad, seconded on trial from the local force. He was the same age as the girl who had been murdered.

'Did you go to a local school, Dixon?'

'No, sir, I went to school in Exeter.'

'Did you make the sixth form?'

'One year, sir, I wasn't up to "A" levels.'

'I've got a job for you, visiting some of the schools.'

Dixon did his best to express keen attention from his curly blond hair to his shining toe caps. Although he was in plain clothes he still wore regulation shoes.

'I've been looking at the Education Year Book. There are seven comprehensive schools in the city, four of which were once grammar schools. There are also two direct-grant schools with sixth forms. I want you to take along a photograph of the dead girl and find out which school she attended; also, what her name was.'

'Her name, sir?'

'Unless I'm mistaken, it wasn't Lily Painter.'

'No, sir, I understand.'

'Remember, girls change a lot in nine years, between seventeen and twenty-six. It might help you to know that she had a good crop of "O" and "A" levels.'

'University?'

'Probably not.'

DC Fowler was an older man, forty-five. He had remained a DC because he had consistently failed the examination for sergeant but he was a good jack of the old breed, slow and dogged. His briefing was simpler. To find the owner of 9 Stanley Street. 'I don't want you to approach him, just find out who he is and anything else you can without creating a fuss.'

At the council offices Fowler found that the rates on 9 Stanley Street were paid by a firm of estate agents, Farley, Roscoe and

Bates, on behalf of the owners; and the owners were given as the City Property Trust. Farley, Roscoe and Bates had a reputation for shady deals but they had never yet faced criminal proceedings.

Fowler satisfied himself that the City Property Trust did not appear in the telephone directory then he went along to the offices of the estate agents.

The usual shop window full of cards and photographs advertising properties for sale. An outer office with a languid blonde who had difficulty in summoning enough interest to find out what he wanted, but in the end he was shown into Mr Bates' private office.

Bates was a tubby little man in a blue pin-striped suit that was too small for him. He had a cold and spoke with a paper tissue held to his nose. 'No, Mr Fowler, we are not the City Property Trust, we merely act for them as we do for other clients—rents, rates, repairs, tenancy agreements and so forth.'

'Who is the tenant of 9 Stanley Street?'

Bates looked a little shocked. 'Really, Mr Fowler, you cannot expect me to—'

'She was strangled last night, as I expect you saw in this morning's paper.'

Bates removed the paper tissue long enough to sneeze. 'Dear me. Strangled. In that case you must surely know who she is.'

'We would like your confirmation.'

Bates stood up, though his legs were so short it made little difference, and went to a filing cabinet. He extracted a thickish file with his free hand, put it on the desk and riffled through the pages. 'Here we are, 9 Stanley Street, a tenancy agreement between Miss Lily Painter and the Trust entered into three years ago. I'm sorry that she has...' He seemed to find difficulty in ending the sentence and gave up.

'You knew her?'

'Oh, no, I never met the lady but she was a good tenant. A money order on the nail, the first day of every month.'

'A money order?'

'Always. Some people are funny like that, especially the ladies, they don't like cheques.'

'How much?'

Bates sniffed loudly. 'I beg your pardon?'

'The rent—how much?'

'I certainly cannot disclose such information about a client.'

'Don't strain yourself.' Fowler's stare

was contemplative rather than aggressive. 'I'll just assume the rent was enough to tell you the place was being used as a brothel.'

'A *brothel?*'

'Premises where two or more prostitutes follow their trade. Your tenant was a prostitute and she sub-let to another.'

Bates took time off to search for a fresh tissue and to dispose of the old one. 'If what you say is true it is a matter for the owners, I am merely their agent.'

'So we had better get to the owners. The City Property Trust do not appear in the telephone book.'

'I could give you their address.'

'Good.' Fowler waited with his pencil poised.

'They have an office at 24 Middle Street.'

'And an ex-directory telephone number, I expect. What is it?'

'As far as I know they have no telephone. Our only contact with them is through the post.'

'What other rents do you collect for them?'

Bates looked scandalized. 'Now you

really are going outside your brief, Mr Fowler.'

'All right. Any other properties in Stanley Street?'

Bates hesitated, then decided to accept the compromise. 'Numbers fifteen and twenty-two.'

'Both converted into flats?'

Bates was distinctly unhappy but he answered. 'Number fifteen has been converted but twenty-two is occupied by an elderly couple.'

'Who just won't die or get out—annoying for you. What do you do? Put fireworks through their letter-box or pay young thugs to break their windows?'

Bates stood up. 'Mr Fowler! You have no right to insinuate anything of the kind. I shall—'

'The rents you receive on behalf of the Trust—where do you bank them?'

'We don't. The money is sent to the Middle Street office.'

'Including cheques?'

'Including cheques.'

'Thank you, Mr Bates, we shall be in touch again.'

Fowler went back to his car and reported over the radio. After a brief wait he received instructions to take a look at the Middle Street premises. 'Mr Gill says you're to use your discretion, don't stir anything.'

'Which means,' Fowler interpreted, 'whatever happens I'm left holding the sticky end.'

Middle Street was a street of small shops not far from the city centre. It had largely escaped the wartime bombing and, until now, the devastation of the planners. But it was obviously ripe: two or three shops were boarded up having fallen into the hands of speculators who were biding their time. Fowler could dimly remember this street before the war. On Saturdays it had been closed to traffic and market stalls ran the length of the roadway. On Saturday nights it was like a fairground with cheap-jacks, quack doctors and buskers competing for the hard earned sixpences and shillings of their customers. All in the glare of spitting arc lamps.

Number twenty-four was a tobacconist's but there was a side door with a large letter-box labelled, City Property Trust. No bell. Fowler went into the shop where a fat man stood with his elbows on the counter reading a newspaper.

'City Property Trust?'

The fat man shook his head without looking up. 'Nothing to do with me.'

'There's no bell.'

'That's right. It wouldn't be much use if there was—there's nobody there most of the time.' His attention was still on the newspaper.

Fowler produced his warrant card. 'I want to get in touch with whoever runs it—when are they there?'

The tobacconist straightened up. He was a man of few words. 'They come and go.'

'When?'

'Afternoons mostly, of course, I wouldn't know about evenings and Sundays.'

'Who are they?'

'Search me.'

'You must have seen them.'

He shook his head. 'No, they come in the back way and I don't have a back entrance.' He kicked the door behind him which opened into his stockroom. 'You can see for yourself.'

Fowler saw. At the back of the stockroom a window fitted with fluted glass and, behind it, the blurred outline of a staircase like a fire-escape going diagonally across the window.

'I think it's a woman mostly—light footsteps, but sometimes there's more than one and I've heard a man's voice.' He showed a first sign of curiosity. 'What they done?'

'Nothing as far as we know, we want to get in touch with them about one of their tenants.'

'Then your best plan is to go to the agents, Farley, Roscoe and Bates, that's where I pay my rent.'

As Fowler was leaving he added, in a burst of confidence, 'Three or four times when I've come here late of an evening I've heard somebody moving about upstairs.'

'Thanks.'

Fowler again reported over his car radio.

'Which gets us no further,' Wycliffe said when the news was passed on to him. He was standing in the big window of his office looking out over the garden which had been contrived in a vain attempt to make the crudity of the new buildings acceptable. Grass, geometrical beds and unlikely rockeries—not a tree. Public officials have tree phobia. Beyond the sparse oasis a main highway ran north out of the city. The rain was falling vertically out of a leaden sky.

He turned to Gill who was sprawled in the customer's chair, smoking. 'Anything else?'

'Records have matched one set of prints found in the Stanley Street flat. They belong to Martin Arthur Salt, a former bookmaker, of 3 Lavington Place, sent down for fraud in '67. He served twenty-seven months of a three year sentence. I've got his file here.' Gill passed a folder across the desk and Wycliffe leafed through it idly.

The usual photograph which would make the archangel Gabriel look like an old lag. A thin face, deep-set eyes and a twisted nose. Thinning hair. Date of birth 27.2.30. Addresses of betting shops in the city and neighbouring towns which formed his empire. A list of pubs he frequented and one club. According to the file he had been suspected of running a protection racket with the help of two strong-arm boys but the fraud charge was all they could make stick.

Wycliffe closed the file with a sigh. 'Where is he now?'

Gill heaved his bulk forward to stub out a butt end. 'He's back at Lavington Place doing very nicely.'

'On what?'

'On the money stashed away in his wife's name before he was nobbled. I wouldn't mind doing bird for a couple if it meant I could live easy for the rest of my natural.' Gill maintained that crime paid and never missed a chance to underline his point.

'What about the muscle boys?'

'They were never charged but they both had form. Edward Short—he seems to have pushed off on to somebody else's patch; but the other chap, Peter "Dicey" Perrins, is still around. He seems to have kept his nose clean.'

'I'm sending a crime car to bring in Salt.'

Wycliffe returned to his chair and started to fill his pipe. 'That's reasonable, Jimmy, but don't forget our first job is to find out who this girl was.'

Constable Dixon spent the morning and part of the afternoon going from school to school. Anxious to make a good impression he did not stop for lunch but contented himself with coffee and a sandwich in a snack bar. If he had imagined that getting out of uniform into the CID would give him status, he was disappointed. In only one school did he succeed in reaching the headmaster, in the others he received cursory attention from one of the secretaries between more urgent tasks.

'What did you say her name was? But if you're not sure of her name how can we help you? You can look at the school photographs if you like—they're hanging in the hall.'

'"A" level results for '64? The teacher responsible for examinations is with a class. If you'd like to wait for the bell you might catch him. In about fifteen minutes.'

He struck oil at last in one of the direct-grant schools. A plump, motherly, grey-haired woman in the office looked at his photograph of the dead girl with interest. 'That face is familiar. '64, you say? Nine years ago. Hold on.'

She went away and came back with a ledger-like book. She flicked through the pages. 'Here we are—1964 "A" level results. Abbott, Joyce; Barker, Gwendoline; Bonnington, Celia; Cave, Dawn—Goodness! How it takes you back. We had a good lot of girls that year.' She ran rapidly down the alphabet. 'Christine Powell—that's her.' She followed along the columns with a stubby finger. 'History,

English, French and Art—all with A-grades. She was a very clever girl, there's no doubt about that—but wild–'

'She didn't go to university?'

'No, I'm sure she didn't, though with those grades she could have walked in. Wait a minute...' She went through to another room and came back with a file. 'Here we are, July '64 leavers.' Once more a long list of names. '...Paley, Parker, Powell. She went to the School of Art and Architecture, here in the city, to study art and design, though I doubt if she stayed the course.'

Dixon spread out the newspaper for her to read.

'Got herself murdered—well, I can't say I'm all that surprised. But what a waste. Boy mad she was, even in the third form. Well, poor girl, I suppose she paid for it.'

Dixon asked if the school had her address.

'We shall have her address at the time she left but as far as I know we've had no contact since.'

This time, the Admissions Register. 'Christine Powell, admitted September 1957, left July 1964. Address: 4 Conniston Gardens.'

'Conniston Gardens. They must have had money.'

'Oh, they did. If I remember rightly he was a big noise in the docks. He came in once or twice when the head had occasion to complain of one of Christine's more outrageous escapades. Of course he blamed the school. Not a pleasant man.'

Dixon reported over his car radio. 'Do I follow up at Conniston Gardens?'

After a brief wait he was told to report back.

Assuming the identification of the photograph to be correct, Wycliffe now knew the dead girl's name and could find out about her family. He questioned one of the local men, a sergeant who had nearly thirty years service behind him.

'Conniston Gardens? That would be Sir George Powell, sir. He was chairman of the Docks Board. He and his wife were killed in a road accident six or seven years back.' The sergeant passed a hand over his balding skull. 'Quite a character Sir George, they don't come like him any more. He was chairman of the Watch Committee back in the days of the old city force. A great Methodist with two bees in his bonnet: drink and sex.' The sergeant frowned. 'I can't recall a daughter but there was a son, all set to follow in father's footsteps. I don't know what happened to him.'

Well, it shouldn't be difficult to find out. Wycliffe had an odd feeling about the case. he was convinced that it was not a sex crime. But what? Did it mean anything that she had had a good education and wealthy parents? Why should it? She was a whore like any other.

A genteel tap on the door and the deputy chief came in. Hugh Annesley Bellings, the next chief constable, if diplomacy and friends meant anything.

'There you are, Charles.' Bellings always made his greeting sound as though he had run his quarry to earth after a long and tiresome chase. 'May I?'

He parked his slim bottom on the customer's chair, crossed his elegant legs and placed long, thin fingers tip to tip. One major snag in the recent move was having Bellings down the corridor instead of half-way across town.

'This murder, Charles, I find it very disturbing.'

'All murders disturb me.' Wycliffe came away from the window and sat in his chair.

'Of course, but the implications of this one are particularly unpleasant. It could well be the start of a series. This type of crime–'

Wycliffe felt like asking 'What type of crime?' but held his peace.

'Lily Painter, wasn't it?'

'Her real name was Powell, she was using a false name.'

'Indeed.'

'Christine Powell, she was the daughter of a chap killed in a road accident, a former chairman of the Docks Board.'

'But I gathered from the reports that she was a—'

'A common prostitute—she was.'

Bellings looked shocked and Wycliffe smoked his pipe in silence.

'But this is incredible. George Powell—well, I won't say that he was a friend but we met socially. He was chairman of the Watch Committee. As a matter of fact I'm still in touch with his son. I've never come across the girl but I do remember hearing some distasteful rumours. What a tragedy. The family seems to be dogged by misfortune—calamity one might say.'

'You mentioned the son.'

'Jonathan, what about him?'

'I need to get in touch, I must confirm the identity of the corpse if nothing else.'

Bellings forced his attention back to the police aspects of the case. 'Yes, of course.'

'Is he still here?'

'Oh, no. When his parents were killed he sold the place in Conniston Gardens and moved to London.'

'How does he earn his living?'

Bellings pursed his lips before answering. 'He's connected with a large property syndicate. George Powell died a rich man and Jonathan is no fool. From what I hear he hasn't been losing money over the past few years.'

Bellings reflected on a fate which was no respecter of persons. 'I'll telephone him. The poor fellow will be distrait.'

'I think I'd better do that.'

'What? Oh, yes, I suppose so. But do be careful, Charles.' He smiled. 'We really are in the big league with this one.'

'His address?'

'I'll phone it through.'

'Is he married?'

'Jonathan? No, he's a bachelor, confirmed I should say.'

When Bellings had gone Wycliffe telephoned the School of Art and Architecture. Although term had ended the principal was still there and agreed to see him.

The school was housed in a Victorian building with a stucco front and pillared entrance opposite the city polytechnic, a mushroom growth of glass and concrete approaching skyscraper proportions. The poly made the old building look squat, shabby and apologetic, like an elderly poor relation.

He was received in an office that had been carefully planned in every detail of furnishing and decoration to suggest a middle-of-the-road establishment that kept, nevertheless, an intelligent eye on the future. A couple of framed paintings were 'early modern' in conception, there were framed architectural drawings of unexceptionable taste and a little bronze confection on a plinth with lots of spikes to point the way ahead. Too little or too much and the purse strings might tighten. There was no notice saying 'No pot here' but the point was being made. No polythene fun tents either.

'Mr Slater?'

They shook hands. The principal had a

regulation haircut except for sideburns and he wore a corduroy jacket.

'As you know, I would like to hear what you can tell me about Christine Powell, the girl who was murdered.'

Mr Slater consulted a folder which lay on his desk. 'She came to us in 1964 to study Art and Design—at that time, a two year course intended to prepare students for work in industry. There was a choice of specializations in the second year.'

'You remember Christine?'

'Of course.'

'What sort of girl was she?'

'As a student she showed unusual ability...'

'As a person?'

The manicured fingers stroked a carefully shaved chin. 'There were problems.'

'Such as?' Wycliffe shifted irritably in his chair. 'I am not asking you for a testimonial, Mr Slater. The girl was brutally murdered and I have to find out everything I can about her that might have a bearing on her death.'

Slater decided to force himself. 'She was a very difficult girl to deal with; she resented every attempt to bring her into any degree of conformity.'

'To what was she expected to conform?'

Slater looked disapproving. 'To reasonable standards of conduct.' Wycliffe's silence forced him to continue. 'Her behaviour was often outrageous and she lost no opportunity of rendering herself conspicuous. Had it not been for her father's influence I am sure that my governors would have expelled her during her first term.'

'Did she complete the course?'

'She did not.'

'What happened?'

Slater looked faintly embarrassed. 'She was expelled.'

'Despite her father?'

'As a matter of fact the final outrage occurred after the crash in which he was killed.'

'What was this outrage?'

'She attended a founder's lecture, a semi-public occasion, in the nude.' Perhaps Wycliffe did not look suitably shocked for Slater added with asperity. 'These things matter in an institution which depends on public funds.'

'I'm sure they do. Why did she do it?'

'Why did she do it? Why do exhibitionists exhibit themselves? The excuse was that she

65

did it for a bet.' Mr Slater placed the folder in a drawer of his desk. 'A great pity, she was very talented.'

'Had she any special friends?'

'There were a good many who enjoyed her notoriety at second hand. Towards the end of her stay here she did make one friend, a young man called Morris—Paul Morris. He was studying architecture and he was one of the most able pupils we have ever had. He was a retiring young man, introspective and shy, so their association was really quite remarkable and, to me, inexplicable.'

'What happened to him?'

'He qualified, of course, and he now works for Lloyd and Winter, here in the city. I've no doubt that he will go far.'

Back in his office Wycliffe telephoned Jonathan Powell at the number Bellings had given him. There was no reply and he gave instructions for the operator to keep trying. Then he telephoned Lloyd and Winter and asked to speak to Paul Morris. He was put through without difficulty.

Morris sounded abrupt and distant. If he was going to translate imagination and skill on the drawing board into commercial success he would have to do something about his manner on the telephone. But he readily agreed to come to the police headquarters in the afternoon.

'At two o'clock, Mr Morris, thank you.'

Morris had not asked why his attendance was required.

Half past twelve. Sixteen hours since Lily Painter or Christine Powell had been strangled. She had not been killed by a psychopathic nut on the loose. The evidence was against it. The missing keys, the methodical stripping of the body after death and the orderly placing of the girl's clothes. The murderer had tried, clumsily, to cover his tracks by simulating the trappings of a sex crime.

The commoner motives for murder are greed or fear or both. It seemed unlikely that anyone would profit financially from the death of Lily Painter though the possibility could not be ruled out. There was certainly money in the Powell family. Did someone fear her enough to kill her? Prostitutes, especially high class ones, are often in a position to blackmail, and relentless blackmail can be a powerful spur to violence though, in practice, it rarely follows.

Wycliffe sighed and lit his pipe. WPC

Saxton opened the door of his office. 'It's time for my lunch, sir.'

'What? Yes, of course, you run along.'

She hesitated. 'Aren't you—?' But she broke off in mid-sentence and closed the door quickly. Strange girl.

There was a complication. Who had been murdered? Lily Painter or Christine Powell? The girl had led a double life and he knew little of one and nothing of the other. Yet it was one of his maxims; 'Know your victim'. He must practise it now. But which one had been killed? Which one?

Wycliffe soon tired of speculative thought, his ideas clouded and his mind became confused, he would find himself repeating a particular word or phrase over and over again like a record caught in a groove. He knocked out his pipe and went down the corridor in search of Gill.

He found him with Martin Salt the ex-bookmaker and con-man whose prints had been found in the dead girl's flat. Salt was sandy haired and balding, freckled with a wispy moustache. His nose looked as though it had collected more than one well-directed punch.

'You know why you are here, Mr Salt?'

'Mr Gill has been telling me.'

'Well?'

'What do you expect me to say? That my wife doesn't understand me?'

'If she did she probably wouldn't pay the bills.'

Salt was not in the least put out. 'You're hard on me, Mr Gill. As you know, I'm unemployed.'

Wycliffe took his time over lighting his pipe. 'Apart from the obvious what was your relationship with the dead girl?'

Salt sighed. 'I know better than to fence with you chaps so let's get this straight. I visited Lily once a week; she was accomodating and there it ended. She was a nice kid, I liked her.'

'You called her Lily?'

'What do you think I call a girl I'm in bed with? Miss Painter?'

'Her real name was Christine Powell.'

'So? The chick wore a phoney label. I don't blame her in that racket. Perhaps her family didn't care for it, some people are funny that way.'

'She was George Powell's daughter, the chap who was chairman of the Docks Board.'

Salt seemed to find this highly amusing.

'The holy docker? Christ! he would have gone for that.'

'You didn't know?'

'I'll say I didn't, but it's bloody funny. He was a regular Bible basher. Hot on vice too.' He laughed loudly. 'It's bloody funny to think of it, isn't it?'

'Very funny but I wouldn't laugh too soon.'

'You've got nothing on me, Mr Wycliffe.'

Wycliffe smiled. 'Do you know anything of the City Property Trust?'

Salt took a cigarette from his case and lit it. 'I've heard of them but I know nothing about the set-up.'

'Do you know who runs it?'

'Surprise me.'

'You don't happen to be involved yourself?'

'Me? I've no money as you should know.'

'Your wife, then?'

Salt blew a perfect smoke ring and watched it rise. 'I doubt it, but Mavis plays her cards pretty close to her chest these days—if you'll forgive the expression.'

Gill came to stand by Salt. 'You've got form.'

'Don't I know it.'

'Just remember, anything we find out that you haven't told us... You get the message?'

'Oh, I got the message in the first place, Mr Gill. When it's an open field you lean on anybody you can. Can I go now?'

Wycliffe intervened. 'Don't be impatient, Mr Salt. Do you know any of the other regulars at Stanley Street?'

'Sorry.'

'When were you last there?'

'Friday, that's my day.'

'So, if somebody said they saw you coming away from the flat on Wednesday evening, they would be lying?'

'*If* somebody said so. I've got a twenty-two carat alibi for Wednesday evening.'

'Save it, you may need it,' Wycliffe said grimly.

Salt looked put out. 'What's that supposed to mean?'

Wycliffe ignored the question. 'A regular visitor at Stanley Street with the initials JH.'

Salt was about to deny any knowledge but changed his mind. 'JH, you say, it's possible...'

'What is?'

'That your JH could be Jimmy Harkness.'

'Who is he?'

'He's a surveyor and valuer in a fairly big way of business.' Salt passed a hand over his thinning hair. 'I don't know, of course, but I've heard that he's always willing to give a helping hand to a working girl.'

'Have you ever seen him there?'

'Sorry.'

'Has Christine Powell ever mentioned him?'

Salt shook his head. 'Never.'

'Then what have you got against him?'

Salt looked pained. 'You asked for a name, Mr Wycliffe. I've got nothing against Jimmy Harkness but I don't owe him either. If he was mixed up in this business I'd just as soon he didn't get away with it.' Self-righteous. 'Can I go now?'

'If you like.'

As Salt reached the door Wycliffe said, 'If you see Dicey Perrins around, give him my regards. We are old acquaintances.'

Salt turned to face the superintendent. He was about to say something but changed his mind and went out.

'We didn't get a lot out of him.'

72

Gill lit a cheroot. 'There's more to come, I'll screw him next time. What did you make of the bit about this chap Harkness?'

'He's got a grudge obviously but there could be something in it. Discreet enquiries.'

CHAPTER THREE

Among the reports which had come in as a result of house-to-house enquiries in the Stanley Street area was one from a woman who lived in Waterloo Place, a quiet street of small houses often lined with parked cars. She had gone up to her bedroom to fetch something and had happened to look out of the window. She had seen, some way down the street, a man in a grey overcoat trying to unlock the door of a parked car. She had noticed him because he seemed to be having difficulty and twice he had dropped his keys into the gutter.

'You hear so much about cars being stolen these days, I wondered. But as far as I could see from that distance, he looked a respectable body so I thought he must be just plain clumsy.'

'What sort of car?'

'Oh, it was a Mini.' She laughed. 'The only kind of car I can recognize. I can't tell you the colour exactly because the light from those street lamps is so queer but I think it was blue.'

'New or old?'

'How would I know? It seemed to go all right.'

'You saw him drive away?'

'Oh, yes. He went off down the street. He seemed a bit careless.'

'Careless?'

'As though he couldn't steer straight or something. I remember wondering if he was drunk.'

'What about the man himself? tall? short? young?'

'Well, I couldn't see very well and I wasn't paying that much attention; I mean, you don't, do you? But he wasn't short. I suppose he must have been tall because he had to stoop quite a bit to fit the key in the lock of the car door. As to his age, well, he wasn't old—not really old, but I can't say more than that.'

'Shabby or smart?'

She shook her head. 'The overcoat looked all right but that's all I can say. He was slim, I'd swear to that.'

Brenda had spoken of Daddy as wearing a grey overcoat.

Another list. The owners of all blue or

green Minis registered in the city and the county. Of course the car could have been registered anywhere in the country but one had to start somewhere. According to the traffic department the list was likely to run to four or five hundred names and it would certainly take a long time to prepare.

The enquiries among tailors and out-fitters had been unproductive. Grey tweed overcoats seemed to have been purchased by half the male population of the city. Even the bespoke tailors had long lists. Still, it had to be done. Turn every stone. That's detection.

At two o'clock Wycliffe had gone out for a snack lunch and the architect, Paul Morris, was shown into Gill's office. He was tall, almost as tall as Gill, thin, pale, with black hair cut short and he was sombrely dressed in pepper-and-salt gent's suiting. 'On sale or return from a seminary,' was Gill's unspoken comment.

'Sorry to drag you up here, Mr Morris, wasting good drinking time.'

Morris sat where he was bidden but he did not smile. 'I was told that you thought I might be able to help with a certain enquiry.'

'That's right, any idea which?'

Morris was finding it difficult to keep his voice steady. 'I suppose you are investigating the death of the girl whose photograph appeared in the paper.'

Gill nodded, grinning. 'Right first time. She was murdered actually—strangled. Somebody got their hands round her neck and squeezed the life out of her—literally. A brooch she was wearing was forced into her neck until it brought blood. Nasty.'

Morris said nothing.

Gill lit a cheroot. 'You knew her?'

The young man was holding himself in with difficulty, his hands were clasped tightly between his knees. 'The newspaper did not give her right name.'

'Oh. What was she called then?'

'Her name was Powell—Christine Powell.'

'But you recognized her photograph in spite of the wrong name?'

He stared at the floor and spoke in a low voice. 'I tried to persuade myself that it was someone else.'

'But now you're convinced that it wasn't. That's something. How well did you know her?'

'Quite well.'

'How well is quite? Well enough to go to bed with her?'

'I did not go to bed with her.'

Gill looked surprised. 'Why not? Everybody else did. You queer or something?'

Morris coloured. 'You have no right to say such a thing. I—'

'When did you last see her? Was it yesterday evening?'

'No, I didn't see her yesterday evening. The last time—'

'What were you doing yesterday evening, Mr Morris?'

'I was at the office until six then I had a meal and after that I spent the evening at Andrew Jarvis's—the Old Custom House. I left there about ten.'

'No home to go to?' When Morris did not answer he went on, 'Who's this Andrew Jarvis? You'll have to spell everything out for an ignorant copper.'

'You know the Old Custom House?'

'A great barn of a place in Bear Street, some sort of second-hand bookshop.'

'Actually it's an antiquarian bookshop run by Jarvis. He has his own bindery and he does a lot of restoration work for libraries and museums.'

'Good for him. Where do you fit in?'

Morris took out his handkerchief and blew his nose. Afterwards he continued to hold the handkerchief in his hand, rolled up in a ball. 'Jarvis has turned one of the attics into a studio and I go there to paint.'

'Why?'

'Why? Because I have no facilities at home.'

'What does he get out of it?'

Morris made a grimace of distaste. 'He gets nothing out of it, he likes to help people who, in his opinion, have some talent. He sells pictures painted by local artists at a small commission.'

'So you spent yesterday evening there painting. I thought you chaps only worked in daylight?'

'I have to paint when I can.'

'Do you spend much time there?'

'Two or three evenings a week.'

'And week-ends?'

'Very often—yes.'

'And the chick—did she ever go there with you?'

'Sometimes, she is interested in painting.'

'Was.'

'I beg your pardon?'

'She *was* interested, she's dead—remember? Where and when did you meet her?'

'We met at an Arts Society meeting

several months ago. She isn't a regular member but she came to hear a particular speaker.'

Gill studied the boy closely. 'You married?'

'No, I live with my mother who is a widow.'

'Anybody to support your story?'

'What story?'

'That you spent yesterday evening painting pictures. Was there anybody in the studio with you?'

'No, Andrew was there when I arrived but he had to go out and I was alone after that but it's absurd to think—'

'I don't think anything but I've got a different version of how you came to meet the girl.'

'A different version? I don't understand—'

'That you met her when you were both at the School of Art together—years ago.'

'But that's true. The point is we met again after not seeing each other for years.'

'Is it true that she got herself expelled?'

'In a way.'

'For coming to a lecture starkers?'

'It was a rag.'

Gill shook his head in mock solemnity,

'She doesn't sound your sort of girl to me.'

Morris was needled. 'I don't see how you can possibly know what "my sort" of girl is.'

Gill grinned ferociously. 'No but we've plenty of time to get better acquainted.' He stared at the young man and puffed smoke across the desk. 'Did she ever take you home?'

'Home?'

'To Stanley Street.'

'I didn't know she had a flat there until I saw the paper.'

Gill thought this might even be true. 'She ran a very profitable business from the flat in Stanley Street, she was a sort of high class call girl.'

Morris flushed. 'You can't expect me to believe that.'

'Suit yourself. When did you last see her?'

'On Sunday at Jarvis's.'

Gill crushed out his cheroot and sat back in his chair. 'So you were at Jarvis's studio from, say seven-thirty until about ten, last night—is that right?'

'Yes.'

'You spoke to Jarvis before he went out,

was he back when you left?'

'No.'

'What about locking up?'

Morris looked surprised. 'I forgot—Derek was in the house all the time, I told him when I was going and, incidentally, he looked in for a word during the evening.'

'Derek?'

'Derek Robson, he's Jarvis's assistant and he lives on the premises.'

'You say he looked in to see you—when?'

'Not long after Andrew left, say a bit before eight.'

They sat in silence while the hand of the wall clock jerked forward three or four times, each time making a little click. When Gill spoke again his manner had changed, he was ingratiating, inviting confidences. 'What sort of girl did you *think* she was?'

'I don't know what you mean.'

Gently. 'Of course you do. Would you have married her if you'd had the chance?'

'There was no question of that.'

'Why not? Did you ask her?'

Morris stared dumbly at the top of the desk. There was no need for him to speak; the fact that the girl had noticed him had been enough, he had never aspired to more than that. Occasionally he had been allowed the privilege of her company. Gill, who assumed that all women would dance to his tune, made an involuntary grimace of distaste which was not lost on Morris.

'What did you like about her?'

Morris was silent for a while but he answered at last, 'She was very intelligent, very talented—', then he saw the look on Gill's face and stopped.

'Have you got a car, Mr Morris?'

'Yes, why?'

'A blue Mini?'

Morris looked concerned. 'Yes, why?'

'Did you have it at Jarvis's place last night?'

'Yes...'

'A man, tall, thin, wearing a grey overcoat and driving a blue Mini was seen near the Stanley Street flat at about the time of the crime. Have you got a grey overcoat?'

'Yes but there must be scores—'

'Hundreds.' Gill scowled grotesquely. 'Don't go away without letting us know, Mr Morris. Happy Christmas.'

Morris did not answer but he got up from his chair looking dazed.

'I expect you can find your own way out.'

When Wycliffe returned from his lunch Gill told him of his interview with Morris. 'Innocents like that are dangerous when they get away from mother—nobody to tell them right from wrong.'

Wycliffe was amused to hear that Morris was a regular visitor at the Old Custom House. 'You probably don't know this chap Jarvis; apart from running the antiquarian bookshop, he sells pictures painted by favoured local painters. Unless I'm mistaken he's an old queen. Helen and I were there a few weeks back looking at his paintings and we bought one for the new house. I think I might renew his acquaintance.'

With the visit in mind, Wycliffe collected his car from the car park and drove through the city centre in the direction of his home. About half-a-mile beyond the centre he turned left off the main road, parked his car on a meter, and walked down a narrow cobbled alley which took him to what had once been the maritime heart of the city. Now it was a picturesque backwater mummified for tourists. The sunshine was deceptive, the air was crisp and cold, there would certainly be a heavy frost before nightfall.

Three or four fishing boats still made a living out of the harbour, a few pleasure craft plied for hire in the summer and a score of shops along the waterfront sold antiques, pictures, Scandinavian rugs and furniture, way-out kitchen equipment and 'gifts'.

Perhaps the fishing boats had been out all night and had long since landed their catch, perhaps the owners of the pleasure craft were pursuing their winter occupations elsewhere, perhaps if he had not come in the slack of a week-day afternoon the shops would have been teeming with with discerning customers clamant for a Redouté chopping board or a tea towel with a recipe for mead printed on it in Gothic characters. Perhaps. But now the harbour was dead. One man in blue overalls and a peaked cap was leaning on the quay rail smoking his pipe while a dog sniffed hopefully round the bollards.

Wycliffe strolled along by the shops until he reached the little square which was used as a car park but even here there was only a single car in the score of spaces which had been marked out. Fronting on the square and facing the harbour was the Old Custom House while to the left, Bear Street pursued its narrow and devious way back to the modern city. The Custom House was two storeys high with attics above and the upper storey jutted out over the pavement supported on pillars. A painted board slung between two of the pillars read: The Jarvis Book Shop—Antiquarian Books a Speciality.

There was no proper shop window but through high sash-windows under the arches made by the pillars it was possible to see rows of books in the dimly lit interior. A sign hung inside the glass panel of the door: Back Shortly. Wycliffe tried the handle of the door but it was locked.

On his earlier visit Wycliffe had been intrigued but repelled by Jarvis. Helen, his wife, like most women, had a soft spot for queers. After an hour spent in looking at books and pictures Jarvis had been calling Helen, 'Helen' and addressing Wycliffe as 'dear boy'.

Wycliffe made another circuit of the harbour and was diverted for a while by a few herring gulls fighting over an anonymous scrap of carrion. By the time it was over he saw Jarvis unlocking his shop door from the outside. Jarvis was a spruce and agile sixty, medium height, spare, with a smooth skin the uniform colour of old parchment. He wore a fawn, cavalry twill suit, a pearl-grey silk shirt with a red tie and sandals. His hair, elegantly silvered at the temples, contrasted too sharply with his chestnut-brown toupée.

'My dear boy!'

Wycliffe was made much of, taken through the shop between dusty shelves crammed with old books into an office where there was a roll-top desk, a swivel chair and more books in piles on the floor. The place smelt, unpleasantly, of mouldering paper and glue. A coffee pot simmered very gently on a gas ring.

'I do hope I haven't kept you, dear boy. I lunch at a little place round the corner in Bear Street and I'm afraid I stopped talking.' He produced two cups and saucers from a cupboard and poured coffee. 'The food is passable but I can't stand their coffee. Milk? Sugar? No, I never take them myself.' He looked down at his belly as flat as a boy's. 'One fights a rearguard action against the battle of the bulge.'

'You live on the premises?'

'Of course, dear boy.'

'Alone?'

'Except for my assistant, Derek.'

'I'm here on police business about the girl who was murdered.'

'Murdered? What girl?' Jarvis paused with his cup halfway to his lips.

'Don't you read the newspapers or listen to the News?'

'Neither, dear boy, I find them too depressing.' He sipped his coffee with an eye on the superintendent. 'Who was she? Someone I know?'

Jarvis was adopting a pose, carefully choosing his line, he was a born actor and it was second nature to him to dramatize every situation. On the other hand, Wycliffe thought he detected a certain uneasiness.

'A girl called Christine Powell, I think she came here from time to time.'

Jarvis looked solemn, he put down his cup to emphasize that Wycliffe had his undivided attention. 'She did, dear boy. You are right. Young Morris brought her. He was infatuated, poor lad.'

'You didn't like her?'

Jarvis smiled as though caught out in a minor fault. 'Am I so transparent? The truth is, dear boy, she was a whore but our Paul did not know it, he is too inexperienced to read the signs. Why she got her claws into him I've no idea; but women are naturally cruel, don't you think?'

He did not expect an answer and went on, 'Paul has the makings of a painter and I am anxious that he should make the most of his talent.'

'You allow him to use your studio?'

'It's not a question of allowing him, I *persuaded* him to do so. For several years I have usually had one or two young painters under my wing. At the moment, Paul is the only one but probably the most talented I have ever had. You see, dear boy, I have no creative ability myself but I recognize it in others—'

'In what circumstances did he bring the girl here?'

Jarvis drank off the rest of his coffee and poured another. 'For you, dear boy? Sure? Paul leads a lonely life and he has come to regard this place as his second home, he spends most of his free time here. His mother is a widow and though he has never said as much I suspect that she is not easy to live with. Anyway, he met this girl at one of our Arts Society meetings and a week or two later he brought her here.'

'Why?'

Jarvis's eyes widened in exaggerated surprise. 'Why? To show her off, dear boy. He was proud of her. It was touching but not a little embarrassing.'

'Embarrassing?'

'Of course. Distressingly so. How does one feel when a friend proudly displays the gem of his collection and one already knows it to be a fake?'

'I see, difficult for you.'

'Very.' He broke off to look at Wycliffe with birdlike curiosity. 'You don't think he killed her?'

'Do you?'

Jarvis chose to take the question at its face value. 'It's possible. It's possible. Paul is a complex personality, the circumstances of his upbringing—no father and a possessive mother, almost certainly his development was impeded. One might say that he is just reaching intellectual and spiritual maturity—coming into flower, so to speak.'

'And that makes him more likely to murder someone?' Wycliffe could scarcely restrain a smile.

Jarvis was piqued. 'You are teasing

me, dear boy. But the answer to your question is probably yes. Disillusionment in adolescence is always dangerous and from many points of view Paul is an adolescent.'

'Was he here yesterday evening?'

'Yesterday? Yes, he was.' Jarvis fiddled with the silvery hair at his temples. 'He dropped in just as I was going out so I left him to it.'

'You left him here alone?'

'Of course, dear boy, he wanted to work.'

'How much time does he spend here in the run of a week?'

'Three or four evenings, usually.'

'Week-ends?'

'As a rule, yes.'

'What time did you go out?'

'Just after seven-thirty. There was a Russian film on at the Arts Society which I wanted to see.'

'And he was not here when you returned?'

'No, I was late, after eleven.'

'Was your assistant on the premises?'

'Derek? Probably, I don't think he went out.'

On the face of it Jarvis was answering

his questions openly and with welcome objectivity yet Wycliffe felt sure that he was holding something back. Most people have secrets to hide, at least a sensitive area which they do their best to guard. A detective is conditioned to sniff out secrets as a pig hunts truffles, but he can waste a lot of time uncovering petty subterfuges and evasions which have nothing to do with his case. He must exercise judgement.

'Did you know that the girl was Sir George Powell's daughter?'

'The Docks Board chap? You surprise me, dear boy.' But he did not sound very surprised.

'I'd like a word with your assistant; Derek Robson, isn't it?'

'That's right, I'll see if I can find him.'

'Looking for me?' He had probably been listening outside the door but he came in without a trace of embarrassment. A man in his early thirties; slim, tall, too self-consciously elegant in his movements. He wore a black, turtle necked sweater and black slacks. 'I gather we have the law on the premises, I suppose it's about Christine?'

'So you've heard what happened?'

'On the radio this morning. I gather

Andy said that he hadn't; it may be true but I sometimes suspect him of saying things just to be interesting.'

Jarvis smiled weakly.

'I understand that you were here all yesterday evening, Mr Robson?'

He nodded. 'I was.'

'And that you looked in on Paul Morris who was working in the studio?'

'That's right, I did.' There was a Welsh rhythm in his voice and the merest trace of an accident although he did not look Welsh. 'To save you the trouble of asking, that was at twenty minutes to eight, I'd left my pen in the studio and I went to collect it. Does all this mean that poor old Paul is for the hot seat? Could he have done it? I mean, he came to my room just before ten—'

Wycliffe was bland. 'I've no idea who committed the crime, Mr Robson. I'm collecting facts. What was Mr Morris doing when you went into the studio?'

'He was painting—working on that city centre thing.'

'As Christine Powell was a regular visitor here, I suppose you knew her reasonably well?'

A faint smile. 'Oh, you could say

that—definitely.' He stooped to a cupboard where Jarvis kept a stock of crockery and came up with a cup and saucer. He poured himself coffee from the pot which must have been almost cold. 'Paul, Christine and me, you could say that we were all good friends. In his more sentimental moments Andy would call us his children.'

'Can you suggest any reason why somebody might want to kill Christine Powell?'

Robson twisted his face into a comical expression. 'If you'll excuse me saying so, that's a damn fool question about a girl who lived as she did. Some Freudian nut, I suppose.'

'So you knew about Stanley Street?'

'She made no secret of it to me.'

'And to Morris?'

'Ah, there you have a real question. I doubt if she was as frank with Paul. Paul had most of his illusions intact and, for some reason, she was anxious to keep it that way.'

'Where did Morris park his car last night?'

'He usually left it in the square.'

'Just one more question, as far as you know, did Christine Powell live in Stanley

Street or did she have another place?'

'As far as I know she lived there, didn't she?'

Wycliffe thanked him and got up. Jarvis walked with him to the shop door. Outside Wycliffe stood, looking up at the frontage. 'A fine old building, you are fortunate.'

'Not really, I have it on a lease with only two years to run.'

Wycliffe started off along the quay and Jarvis called after him. 'Remember me to your charming wife. Tell her that I am expecting some more pictures and I shall want her to look them over...'

The sun was still shining and the harbour deserted. At the top of the cobbled alley where he had left his car was a different world. A stream of cars, lorries and red buses taking harassed people to places they did not really want to go. Wycliffe manoeuvred his car out of the parking space and joined them.

CHAPTER FOUR

On his return to the office Wycliffe spent an hour going through reports. Among others, information about James Harkness, the surveyor. As yet no official enquiry had been started, a random accusation by a man like Salt is not to be taken too seriously and, apart from that, there was only one thing against him, he had the initials JH, the initials which had appeared in the dead girl's engagement book for Wednesday evening. Was Harkness Daddy? It was certainly possible. According to the report Harkness was in his early fifties, head of a very successful firm of valuers, married but without children and gossip had it that his wife led him by the nose. 'A weedy little man,' Gill called him, 'and his wife would make a good stand-in for Dracula's mother-in-law. She stalks around with two bloody great hounds on a leash, "Down, Major. Heel, Boy."'.

Well, Harkness would keep.

He was on the point of leaving for home

when the switchboard rang to say they had succeeded in getting through to Jonathan Powell's London home. Wycliffe told them to connect him.

A self-consciously refined voice. 'I'm afraid Mr Powell is not at home.'

'When do you expect him back?'

A pause for thought. Evidently Powell discouraged discussion of his movements. 'Mr Powell is away on business.'

Wycliffe became brusque and official and after some hesitation he was given an address of an hotel in the city.

'You mean that he's *here,* staying at the Royal Clarence?'

This was an unexpected development. If Powell had been in the city when his sister was murdered it could be coincidence but it could be something else.

The Royal Clarence was probably the oldest and certainly the most discreet of the city's hotels. It had been the town house of a distinguished 18th-century admiral and though the interior had been remodelled and the building extended, its frontage of mellow red brick with beautifully proportioned sash-windows had not been touched. It stood in a secluded backwater near the boundary of the old city, on the edge of a small public park which had once been the garden of the house.

Wycliffe left his car in the cobbled court next to a lethal looking Aston Martin and entered the dimly lit foyer. An elderly uniformed porter looked at him over steel-rimmed spectacles and asked his business.

'Detective Chief Superintendent Wycliffe. Is Mr Powell in his room?'

'He went up twenty minutes ago, sir, I'll telephone.'

'Don't bother. What number?'

'One-o-three, sir, but—'

But Wycliffe was already half-way up the stairs. The door of one-o-three was slightly ajar and Wycliffe heard a woman's voice. 'We shall be late, Johnny, it's seven o'clock already.'

Wycliffe tapped at the door.

'Just a moment.'

A brief interval and the door was opened by a tall, dark girl wearing a blue silk quilted dressing-gown.

Wycliffe introduced himself and asked to speak to Powell.

'He's in his bath.'

'I'm not, I'm dressing. Who is it?'

The girl shrugged and smiled indulgently. 'You'd better come in. Cigarette?

Drink?' She pointed to a table which carried a fair selection of drinks. Evidently Powell did not practise the self-denial his father had preached. And he had good taste in women. This girl, in her middle twenties, was an aristocrat of her sex, her features were good but her beauty lay as much in a serenity of expression and demeanour. Wycliffe was reminded of what he had read of the well trained *geisha*.

'Do sit down, he won't be long.'

Powell came through from the adjoining room wearing dress trousers and a shirt, but collarless. He was stocky, muscular and heavy featured. All his movements seemed to be unnecessarily vigorous as though he chafed under some barely tolerable restraint. No doubt some journalist had called him a human dynamo. Wycliffe had checked his age, he was thirty-eight, but he looked older. His curly hair was streaked with grey and his eyebrows had lost their sleekness and were becoming bushy. He looked at Wycliffe. 'Did you say police?'

'Detective Chief Superintendent Wycliffe.'

'What's it about?'

Wycliffe glanced at the girl.

'You can say what you have to say.' His manner was blunt without being deliberately offensive. 'Whisky?'

'No, thank you.'

'I think I will.' He poured himself three fingers and splashed a thimbleful of soda. 'Have you seen the papers today, Mr Powell?'

'No, have I missed something?'

Wycliffe produced a print of the photograph which Smith had taken of the dead girl. 'Do you recognize this girl, Mr Powell?'

Powell's manner changed. He took the photograph and examined it under the central light. When he turned to Wycliffe his aggression had gone and he seemed worried, tentative. 'That's my sister. What has she been doing?'

'I'm afraid that I have bad news for you, she was found dead in her flat last night.'

Powell stared at the superintendent, his face expressionless. 'In what circumstances?'

Wycliffe told him. 'I'm afraid that you will have to come to the mortuary to make a formal identification.'

Powell looked down at his shirt and

trousers. 'I'd better get out of this. Sonia!'

The girl had gone into the next room, now she came back. She looked at him and said. 'I heard, I'm very sorry, Johnny.'

'You'd better go on by yourself, take a taxi.'

She put a hand on his arm. 'No, I'd rather stay here.'

'As you like.' He finished his whisky in a single gulp and went back to the bedroom.

The girl looked at Wycliffe and seemed about to say something but changed her mind. Powell came back a few minutes later wearing a grey lounge suit with a fine stripe. 'We will go in my car and I will bring you back here.'

Wycliffe was firm. 'No, we will use mine.'

'Take your coat, Johnny, it is bitterly cold.'

Powell ignored her and stalked out leaving Wycliffe to follow. In the foyer he stopped at the desk and scribbled a number on a pad. 'Ring this number and apologize for Miss Adams and me.'

'Certainly, Mr Powell, at once.'

'We were going out,' he told Wycliffe as they passed through the swing doors.

They drove to the mortuary in silence and Powell went through the ordeal without apparent emotion.

'Are you prepared to make a firm identification?'

'Yes, I am.' His eyes wandered over the other drawers in the white room.

Back in his car Wycliffe said, 'I'm afraid I must trouble you to come to headquarters to make a statement.'

'Tonight? Won't the morning do?'

'Tonight.'

Powell was silent for a while as they drove through rain swept streets. Then he said, 'I suppose you're a pretty good policeman?'

Wycliffe did not answer.

'What makes you do it? What do you get out of it?'

'What makes you buy and sell property?'

Powell laughed shortly. 'That's easy, the money.'

'As an end in itself?'

'No, partly for what it will buy—house, car, boats, good food, service—and freedom, I suppose. Though it's a queer kind of freedom, I work harder than most.'

'You said, partly.'

'So I did. Money means power, the

chance to manipulate people and situations. I enjoy that, so did my father though he wouldn't admit it. He had to find a moral justification for self indulgence—not me.'

Most of the headquarters building was in darkness but lights burned on Wycliffe's floor. He parked his car and the two men went upstairs together. Powell looked round the chief superintendent's office, taking everything in. 'They do you pretty well.'

Wycliffe was secretly annoyed with himself for resenting Powell's rather casual, almost patronizing attitude. And he lost the initiative. Powell settled himself in the customer's chair, offered his cigarettes to Wycliffe and said, 'You told me she was found dead in her flat—what flat?'

'In Stanley Street, off Prince's Street. Didn't you know?'

Powell looked vague and did not answer directly. 'I have had very little contact with Christine since our parents died.'

'You quarrelled?'

'No, there were differences of interest and outlook, also twelve years.'

'When did you last see her?' Wycliffe's manner was curt because Powell irritated him.

Powell ran a finger round the inside of his collar. 'God! It's hot in here.' He was stalling and it was obvious, but suddenly he reached a decision. 'I might as well come straight out with it, I saw her yesterday afternoon.'

'At the Stanley Street flat?'

He nodded.

'Then why did you imply just now that you didn't know of it?'

Powell made a gesture of impatience. 'Does it matter? I suppose I was feeling my way. In any case, I think she's got another place, another flat, perhaps.'

'Where?'

'I've no idea. That will be your business to find out.'

Wycliffe sat at his desk, his clasped hands resting on the blotter, he scarcely moved. Powell was restless, he seemed to be holding himself in, simmering and likely to come to the boil at any moment. Presumably he had suffered a shock but Wycliffe had the impression that he lived most of his life under stress. Release for such a man was usually physical, squash or sex or both.

'I'd better explain. I came down specially to see her. My company has plans for the redevelopment of an area in the city, an area which was scarcely touched by the war. Over the past few years we have been buying everything in that area as it comes on the market—not openly, of course, but through agents. Otherwise the price would have risen against us. We now own about seventy per cent of the properties and all but one of the really key premises. That one we were expecting to come on the market soon and we were ready with a realistic bid; but it was snapped up under our noses.'

'Tiresome for you.'

'And expensive. I suspected a leakage of information and I was right.' Powell took time off to inhale deeply on his cigarette. 'Four days ago I received a letter from my sister offering me the property at a greatly inflated price.'

'Diamond cuts diamond.'

Powell grinned. 'Or dog eats dog. She'd got more of the old man in her than I'd thought. But you can see the fix I was in. A leakage of information is an occupational hazard, but a leakage to my own sister...' He made an expressive gesture with the hand that held his cigarette. 'I don't say that my fellow directors would think that I had double-crossed them but they would certainly assume that I had been indiscreet.

Wycliffe was listening with an expressionless face. He was wondering if Powell ever stood aside to take a good look at himself. 'So you tried to persuade your sister to back down?'

Powell grinned, wryly. 'I'm not in the habit of wasting my breath. No, I told her that my company would buy the property at valuation and that I would make up the difference out of my own pocket.' He shrugged. 'That way I would be off the hook and as far as the money was concerned, well, it would still be in the family.'

'What did she say?'

'She accepted, of course, she is a realist.'

'Your father left you most of his money?'

'All of it. I know what you are thinking and you may be right. Father had no time for Chris, she was a late arrival and a mistake and father took a poor view of mistakes, especially his own. But Chris got several thousand under her mother's will so she wasn't destitute.'

'You mentioned your belief that she had another place...'

Powell tapped ash into the tray on Wycliffe's desk. 'You know the flat in Stanley Street? Of course, you must do. Well, in conversation with Chris it became obvious that she was running quite a business in property and one look at Stanley Street makes it obvious that she wasn't doing it from there. I said as much and she laughed, "This is just a listening post, Johnny boy."'

'A listening post?'

'That's what she said.'

'And what do you suppose she meant?'

Powell stubbed out his cigarette. 'Your guess is as good as mine, but I imagine pillow talk from the right people could be profitable as well as interesting.'

He must have been twelve when his sister was born and they must have shared the same house through most of her childhood, yet he had just come from identifying her body and seemed unmoved.

'Which property did she buy against you?'

He hesitated then shrugged. 'The cat is out of the bag anyway now, I suppose. It was the Old Custom House which fronts on the harbour at the end of Bear Lane. Our scheme is to develop the whole of that area behind the harbour—a mixed development: shops, flats, a garage—nothing ostentatious, no tower blocks; keep the scale of the place.'

'I thought the whole of the harbour came under a preservation order?'

Powell shook his head. 'Only the houses on the wharf.'

Wycliffe stood up to close the interview. 'One more thing, Mr Powell; where were you yesterday evening?'

He was clearly surprised by the question. 'Am I under suspicion?'

Wycliffe's face was bland and blank. 'Well over half the murders investigated turn out to be the work of relatives or very close associates.'

'And I stand to gain, I suppose.' A reluctant grin. 'I spent the evening with friends.'

'With Miss—?'

'Miss Adams, Sonia Adams, yes, she was with me.'

'Where?'

'At the Establishment Club, it's—'

'I know where it is. Thank you, Mr Powell.' He walked with Powell to the top of the stairs. 'Let me know when you intend to leave the Royal Clarence.'

Powell went down the stairs three at a time. Wycliffe looked after him with mixed feelings. He frequently asked himself what he was doing with his life, now a good deal more than half gone. It puzzled and worried him that for people like Powell the question either did not seem to arise or was not urgent. Perhaps he misjudged the man. He returned to his office vaguely depressed.

Now was as good a time as any to talk to Bates, the estate agent. Bates almost certainly knew a good deal more than he had told. Wycliffe asked the switchboard operator to get Bates at his home number and a few minutes later he was put through. A woman took the call, she sounded brusque and prepared to be aggressive.

'Mrs Bates?'

'I'm Mr Bates' housekeeper.'

Bates was not at home, she had no idea when he would be back. He had gone out just after lunch. Often he did not come home until very late.

Wycliffe put on his mackintosh and, careful ratepayer that he was, switched off his office lights. The headlamps of cars on the highway chased fantastic patterns across his walls. It was ten o'clock. He walked down an empty corridor, its peace disturbed by the clacking of a single portable typewriter inexpertly used.

His way home took him through the city centre within a couple of blocks of Middle Street. What Powell had said had made him wonder whether it might have been Christine Powell who came and went so mysteriously at the offices of the City Property Trust. According to the tobacconist it was a woman. He parked his car and walked through the drizzling rain. Middle Street was narrow and poorly lit, none of the shops kept their window lights on after closing time but there was a fish and chip shop half-way along, a blaze of white light. Wycliffe was almost seduced by the smell which brought back vivid, bitter-sweet memories of the midland town where he had spent his green years as a policeman. Only a growing respect for the subtleties of his digestive processes restrained him.

He looked up at the window over the tobacconist's and in the light from the chip shop he could see that they were curtained with some sort of drab stuff. Without any particular reason he walked

111

along the street until he came to a narrow alley which led to a service road between the backs of Middle Street and the goods reception areas of some of the big stores which fronted on the city centre. The Middle Street premises had retained their back gardens and he found the door of number twenty-four. Unlike the others it had been freshly painted and it opened easily on well oiled hinges. The garden area had been paved and a brick path led to the foot of an iron staircase to the first floor where one of the windows had been replaced by a glass panelled door. He climbed the stairs; the glass door was uncurtained and with the help of his pocket torch he could see into a small but modern kitchen with white units against green walls. He pressed the bell-push and heard a bell ringing somewhere in the flat but there was no other response. A black and white cat came padding up the stairs and rubbed round his legs, mewing plaintively. By leaning over the rail of the little balcony where he stood he could just see into the room next to the kitchen. The beam of his torch picked out an elegant looking bed-head and above it a large picture or mural. He went back down the stairs and through the garden, carefully closing the back door behind him.

He returned to his car and started for home but he was uneasy in his mind. There was good reason to connect the City Property Trust with the dead girl, especially since his conversation with Powell, but he needed something more definite before going for a search warrant. In the morning he would probably be able to get his information, discreetly, from whichever of the banks handled the Trust's accounts. Meantime... He was tempted to radio a message for a watch to be kept on the premises but there was little real justification for such a use of manpower. He compromised by giving instructions for the Panda patrols to keep an eye on the place.

A newspaper bill-board in a shop doorway caught his eye, its message streaked by rain, CITY MURDER—LATEST. He wondered what they had found to say, the news that the dead girl had been the daughter of the celebrated Sir George Powell had not been released in time for the final edition.

When he reached home Helen was curled up on the sofa reading a gardening book. The red velvet curtains of the big window were drawn and the record player dispensed a discreetly muted *Lohengrin*. Helen, coming late to the pleasures of music was now addicted to Wagner and the early operas of Richard Strauss.

'You look all in, darling. Have you eaten? There's cold chicken and I can easily cook vegetables or make a salad.'

He said no, but changed his mind after a sherry.

Before going to bed he telephoned Bates' house but the estate agent had not returned. From the housekeeper's manner he suspected that his call had got her out of bed. He dropped the receiver then lifted it again and dialled his headquarters. 'I want the Bates house watched, discreetly. Bates is not there at the moment but I want to know when he returns.'

He fell asleep as soon as he got into bed and was not awakened by the bedside telephone when it rang. Helen leaned over him to answer it and when he took the receiver from her he was still fumbling his way out of a confused dream.

'Wycliffe.'

It was an apologetic duty officer. 'I

114

wouldn't have called you, sir, but you did leave word for us to keep an eye on the premises in Middle Street—'

Wycliffe propped himself up, one elbow digging into his pillow. 'Well?'

'There's a fire, Panda three spotted it—smoke coming from between the roofing tiles. Now it seems that the whole upper floor is alight. The brigade is there and so is Sergeant Barber.'

'What time is it?'

'Just after four. Panda three reported it at 0340 hours, sir.' So they had thought twice about ringing him.

'I'll be along.'

He got out of bed and put on his dressing-gown. Helen looked at him sleepily. 'Are you going out?'

He was honest enough not to say, 'I must'. Barber would have handled it and he would have had a full report in the morning but it was not the same.

'Shall I make you some coffee?'

'I'll make my own, would you like a cup?'

'To be honest, I'd rather go back to sleep.'

He did not make any coffee, instead he took a nip of whisky which tasted like vinegar but took care of the hollowness inside.

The rain had stopped and a pale half-moon sailed above broken cloud. It had turned colder.

He drove to the end of Middle Street, parked his car and walked down. The street was cordoned off and he was challenged by a uniformed constable. He had not been in the city long enough to be known to the whole force.

Flames were coming out of the windows above the tobacconist's shop and licking back over the roof; smoke and sparks rose high into the sky. Hoses were directed on to the flames and on to adjoining roofs. Firemen were helping owners of neighbouring houses with the removal of their goods. Pusey, the chief fire officer, was there in faultless uniform, standing by one of the pumps. He nodded to Wycliffe, they had met at a recent civic bunfight.

'What brings you out?' Pusey shouted above the noise of the engines.

'Curiosity. Nobody inside?'

Pusey shook his head. He had a weighty, portentous manner. 'I hope not. It was well alight when our chaps got here. I've got two appliances in the access road between this and the city centre so we are attacking from both sides. I can't afford to take risks in a high density area like this.'

They were interrupted by the fat tobacconist. 'I could have got half my bloody stock out while you've been here arsing about.'

His shop, so far, seemed untouched by the fire but thousands of gallons of water must have streamed down through and it was running in a miniature river out of the front door.

'Don't be absurd! You couldn't possibly go in there. Apart from anything else there is a risk of total collapse.'

'Bullshit. Give you chaps a bit of braid and you think you're the bloody army.'

'A dissatisfied customer,' Wycliffe said as the tobacconist lumbered off.

'Surly oaf,' Pusey grumbled.

Although it was four o'clock in the morning the police had their hands full keeping spectators out of the street. Men and women wearing overcoats or mackintoshes over their night clothes, some with children, stood staring, their faces blank.

'They can't all live round here,' Wycliffe said.

Pusey was disdainful. 'It's a free show.'

Sergeant Barber came to report to Wycliffe. 'Sorry, sir, I've only just heard that you were here.'

The fire had taken hold in the roof timbers and tiles were splitting with gunshot cracks showering fragments down into the street; but the great quantity of water being poured into the building was beginning to have its effect—there was less flame though more smoke and steam. It rose in a lurid column to spread out in a black pall held by the quiet air.

'You seem to be winning,' Wycliffe said.

'Appearances may be deceptive.' And as though to justify Pusey's words there was a sudden rending of timber as the floors of the upstairs front rooms collapsed into the shop below.'

The glass in the shop windows seemed to explode outwards spraying the street with thousands of tinkling fragments. The fire, freshly supplied with air and an abundance of fuel leapt joyfully into renewed life. The heat at this lower level drove the firemen back and even the appliances had to be moved.

In the instant when the floors collapsed

Wycliffe had glimpsed two firemen through a doorway into one of the upstairs back rooms. Pusey had seen them too and he was both concerned and frightened. Wycliffe suspected that he might go to pieces in a crisis. 'Bond should have pulled his men out before this. If anything had happened—'

Wycliffe followed him through the alley into the access road. The contrast was surprising. The back of number twenty-four was still intact, the roof, apparently, little damaged. They picked their way over a tangle of hoses to where Station Officer Bond was standing by his communications van, talking to the man on radio watch.

'Well, are all your men out?'

Bond turned to Pusey—'All out, sir, no casualties.'

Pusey's relief was obvious. 'You ran it fine.'

'Barnes and Pearson were the last two out, sir. They say they saw a body.'

'A body?'

'Barnes is here, sir, he can tell you himself.'

A fireman, his face blackened with soot, his voice hoarse with smoke. 'We didn't see him until just before the floors went.

There was a sort of alcove in the front room which we couldn't see into. As the joists went and the collapse began he came sliding out, what was left of him. Weird. And of course, down he went.'

'A man or a woman?' Pusey demanded.

Barnes reflected. 'I couldn't say, sir. I know I said "he" but that was a manner of speaking. There was not much to go by. You know what they're like after a blaze like this.'

Pusey was looking at Wycliffe with hostility. 'You expected something of the sort.' His manner was an accusation.

'No.'

'You still haven't told me why you are here.'

Wycliffe smiled. 'Do I have to?'

Pusey, a rather dull if conscientious official, was worried. He waved his hand in the direction of the fire. 'You expected this?'

'Certainly not.'

But Pusey wasn't satisfied. 'The head of CID doesn't turn out for fires, even in the city centre.'

Wycliffe was half irritated, half amused. 'I was interested in the premises because of a possible link with a case, but I certainly did not expect that someone would try to burn it down.'

'You are saying that this is arson?'

Wycliffe controlled himself. 'Are you saying that it is not?'

Pusey hesitated then said, 'Come with me.' He led the way across the road to a red van parked in the loading bay of the supermarket. With a key he unlocked the back doors, opened them and shone his torch inside. There was a strong smell of paraffin. The beam of the torch was directed on to a plastic bucket which had a candle inside. The candle was stuck to a square piece of ply-wood and though its wick showed signs of having been lit it could not have burned for more than a few seconds.

Pusey explained. 'An old dodge for starting a fire long after the fire raiser has quit. The ply-wood floats on the surface of the paraffin and when the candle burns down to it—POOF!' He gestured dramatically. 'This one was found in the back bedroom by my men and the candle had probably blown out in the draught caused when the fire raiser opened the back door. I was not first on the scene here but the officer who came with the first appliance told me that there were two distinct centres of combustion in the front of the building, so I conclude that there must have been two more of these. In this one a pair of kitchen steps had been placed astride the bucket and draped with inflammable material. No doubt the others had been treated in a somewhat similar way.'

Wycliffe was recalling his visit of the previous evening at about ten-fifteen. The fire had been spotted by one of his Panda-car men about five hours later. How long did these candles take to burn? It seemed probable that two of the three candles had been burning then. And someone was in the flat, dead or alive.

The collapse of the floors had given no more than a temporary boost to the fire and by the time Wycliffe returned to the front of the premises there were only occasional spurts of flame from the ruins of the shop. The fire was as good as out but it would be hours before it would be possible to search for the body. After he had arranged with Sergeant Barber to set a watch he went to his car. The spectators had thinned and though it was still dark there were already people on their way to work and the streets were coming alive with traffic.

When he arrived at the Watch House he could just see the silvery grey waters of the estuary in a landscape which was still shadowy and mysterious. He left the car in the drive and entered the house by the back door as quietly as possible. In the kitchen he set the percolator going and while it was going through its repertoire he telephoned his headquarters.

'Bates? No, sir, Fowler is watching the place and he reported in half an hour ago.'

So Bates had not returned home during the night and the body of an unknown lay under the smouldering remains of the fire.

He poured his coffee and was perched on the edge of the kitchen table drinking it when Helen came downstairs in her dressing-gown, her eyes puffed with sleep. In twenty years he had never once managed to enter the house without waking her.

CHAPTER FIVE

He had a bath and breakfast. Helen saw that he had what he wanted and kept out of the way. In the early stages of a case he was usually taciturn and, apparently, irritable. In fact, he merely withdrew into himself, cultivating a feeling of detachment and rather enjoying the experience. He listened to the nine o'clock news on the radio. The fact that the dead girl had been the daughter of Sir George Powell had headline rating. The editorial boys had dug up some biographical tit-bits about the man who, in his lifetime, had always been good for mordant, quotable off-the-cuffs about every aspect of manners and morals. Older journalists were inclined to linger over his memory with nostalgic relish. The fire in Middle Street was not mentioned. Why should it have been? Few people knew that a body lay under the debris, fewer still, perhaps only Wycliffe himself, that the pyrotechnics had any connection with the Stanley Street murder. Did he know that they had? He was sure of it anyway.

'I know it's a silly question but have you any idea when you are likely to be home?'

He shrugged without answering. He was watching a tug towing two mud barges through the narrows out to sea. The sea sparkled in the sunshine, the sky was blue with puffy white clouds and the slopes across the estuary were fresh green. The whole thing looked rather like an extravagant water-colour, the choice of colours naïve, childish. One day, when they had time, he and Helen would cross over and explore that headland, follow the coast...

He went to the telephone and dialled his headquarters.

'Bates? Yes, sir. He turned up at his house just after eight. DC Fowler saw him go in. Yes, he was driving a Rover 2000 which he left in the street outside his house. Fowler has been relieved by young Dixon. He's been told to keep in the background.'

So it was not the estate agent's body which had been burned in the fire; but the estate agent had been out all night.

'One more thing, is Inspector Wills there?' Bob Wills was knowledgeable on the subjects of accountancy and business, he spoke the language and he had the advantage of looking like a bank manager.

'Bob?— When the banks open I want you to make the rounds until you find where the City Property Trust banked. The place has been burned down in very suspicious circumstances so you've plenty of grounds. I want to know who signed cheques for the Trust and anything else you can find out about them.'

He got out his car and drove towards the city. In the sunshine the city centre looked like a film set for a Western done in bricks and concrete, low buildings spaced along wide streets, about as cosy as the Gobi desert. He turned off to Middle Street.

Two fire pumps were still there but they were idle and firemen were sweeping muddy water into the gutters. The air was acrid with the smell of charred timber. The ruins of number twenty-four steamed and smoked behind a temporary screen which had been erected to shut out the over-curious. The street remained closed to vehicles but most of the shops were open and loitering pedestrians were being moved on by a constable. Wycliffe went through a wicket in the temporary fence. Sergeant Barber, who must have been almost dropping on his feet, was standing with one of Pusey's men, surveying the ruins.

'They reckon it will be afternoon before we can start, sir.'

Wycliffe looked up to the first floor. Amazingly, the back rooms seemed to be more or less intact. 'Is it safe to go up there?'

The fire officer shook his head. 'Not yet. We are going to shore it up so that it doesn't collapse on us while we clear this lot but what's left of the roof is sagging and it won't be exactly safe even then.'

Wycliffe walked round to the back by way of the alley. The fire appliances had gone from the access road and a huge, articulated lorry had backed into the supermarket loading bay. From a distance the back of number twenty-four looked much the same as it had done before the fire, but in closer view he could see that the door at the top of the steps had been smashed in and that the sashes were missing from the windows. A seagull had chosen that particular roof on which to perch, probably because of the warmth rising from the débris of the fire. It moved crabwise along the ridge, pausing now and then to preen itself or to peer down into the street.

Wycliffe was trying to fit the new developments into some sort of pattern, without much success. If Morris had killed the girl in a frenzy of disillusionment, then what about the fire and body buried under the rubble? Christine Powell's death would probably have precipitated all sorts of crises among her associates and a prudent man among them might want to remove from the Middle Street flat anything which could damage or incriminate him. He might even set the place alight. Bates, Wycliffe thought, was such a man and Bates had been out all night; but the funeral pyre had not been for him.

The firemen were certain that the flat had been locked, back and front, when they arrived; and Christine Powell's keys were missing when her body was found. How had the man (or woman) in the flat died? Had he perished in the fire of his own contriving? It seemed unlikely that he could have been trapped just twelve feet above street level. Suicide was a possibility, perhaps he had killed himself after setting fire to the place. It was equally possible that the dead man had been murdered. Only the post-mortem could give his speculations any substance. Until then—

He was standing in the middle of the narrow access road looking up at the seagull on the roof. The driver of the big articulated lorry shouted at him, 'You thinking to settle there, mate?' He stepped aside and the great shuddering monster, belching diesel smoke, snaked past him. He walked back to his car and drove slowly through the city centre to his headquarters. His driving was always contemplative and, even on motorways, he rarely exceeded fifty.

Back in his office he telephoned Lloyd and Winter, the architects, and asked to speak to Paul Morris. He was put through to Mr Winter.

'Mr Morris is not in today. No, we have had no message. I assume that he is unwell. Chief Superintendent, may I say that I am a little concerned? This is the second time you have been in touch with the office concerning Mr Morris, naturally I am anxious. As a witness, yes, I quite understand. Yes, of course. No, I am afraid that he is not on the telephone at his home.'

Wycliffe gave instructions for a crime car to call at Morris's house and to report back. Then he made a second telephone call, this time to Jarvis at the bookshop.

'I'm sorry to pester you, Mr Jarvis, but I would like to know who leased your premises to you?'

Jarvis was obviously surprised but he made no bones about answering. 'It's no secret. My agreement was with the bookmaker, Martin Salt. That was thirteen years ago, later he transferred his interest to his wife. After that I think he was in trouble with your people.'

'Would it surprise you to know that the reversion of your lease was purchased by Christine Powell shortly before her death?'

'You astonish me, dear boy.' And he sounded as though he meant it. 'Even so, I can't see what it could have to do with—'

'Probably nothing.'

As he put the receiver back on its rest the intercom buzzed. Inspector Wills had made his round of the banks. The City

Property Trust banked with the London and Provincial. All transactions were in the name of Christine Powell. One more loose end gathered in. The manager had said, that to the best of his recollection, Miss Powell had never visited the bank.

A shaft of sunlight had crept round until it was falling across his desk and, for the first time, he noticed a vase of bronze chrysanthemums near the intercom and, as WPC Saxton came in to go through the post, he pointed to them, 'I doubt if the auditor will allow those as a legitimate expense.'

'He won't have to, sir, I brought them.'

He was so surprised he forgot to thank her.

'My father grows them, they are a late flowering variety he developed himself.'

Late flowering. Perhaps WPC Saxton would bloom one day.

Jimmy Gill came in looking, as usual, as though he had slept in his clothes. 'Good morning, sir.' He started the day thus, formally, then felt that he had staked his claim to freedom of speech for the next twenty-four hours. WPC Saxton, knowing that the post would have to wait, retreated and Gill watched her go. He looked her up and down as though he were mentally undressing her, as he was. 'She's not bad, really, pity her hormones don't work.' He sat down in the customer's chair and lit a cheroot. 'So you're having Bates watched?'

'It seemed a reasonable precaution. We don't know where he spent last night.'

'We could ask him.'

'Give him time and he might want to tell us.'

Gill tried a new approach. 'Young Dixon who is keeping obo there reported a few minutes ago over his car radio. He says Bates has been trying to get someone on the telephone for the past hour.'

'How does he know?'

'The main room downstairs runs the full length of the house with a window at each end and Dixon can see in. Every few minutes Bates picks up the telephone, dials, listens for a while then drops it again.'

'I hope Dixon isn't being too clever.'

He brought Gill up to date. When he heard that it was Salt who had leased the Custom House to Jarvis, Gill was intrigued. 'I'll flay that bastard until I get something.' But he admitted that he

133

doubted whether Salt had killed the girl. 'Burning the place down in Middle Street would be more in his line.'

They were interrupted by the telephone. PC Boyd in a crime car had reported over his car radio on his visit to the Morris home.

'Boyd says that Morris did not come home last night.'

'What does his mother say?'

'According to Boyd she's a near nutcase. She seems to have no idea where he is but she's convinced that he's staying away just to upset her.'

'When did she last see him?'

'Yesterday morning when he went to work.'

Wycliffe remembered the graphic words of the young fireman—'he just came sliding out, what was left of him—weird. Of course, down he went.'

'I want his movements traced from the time he left home yesterday morning. Let me know if you need extra help. Try to get a photograph without upsetting his mother, we may need to circulate it.'

Gill was inclined to give a good deal of weight to Morris's disappearance. 'You must admit that there could be a case against Morris. You didn't see the boy, uptight and jumpy as a doe rabbit on heat. He never expected any girl to give him a second look then a real dolly gives him the come-on and he doesn't know what hit him or where. Sir Galahad and the pro'.' Gill's gestures had poetry in them even if his words did not. 'For a few weeks it's stardust and Danny Boy all the way then he comes out of his trance long enough to realize that his holy grail has a few chips out of it. In other words the dolly does and says a few things that aren't in the script and he's worried.' Gill's face wrinkled in sympathy. 'If at that time some busybody passed him the dirt from Stanley Street, all done up in a plain wrapper, then, Bingo! the cork would come out.'

Gill stopped to relight his cheroot which had gone out and Wycliffe watched, mesmerized by the flow of words. 'We've no evidence that he knew anything about Stanley Street until you told him.'

Gill puffed on his cheroot until it was drawing again. 'And no evidence that he didn't.'

'In any case, what about the fire?'

'Suicide.' Gill was rarely at a loss to provide an impromptu explanation of anything. Wycliffe usually discouraged him for, as he said, Gill's ideas contained enough of the truth to confuse the issue.

'You may be right, but we shall know better when they get the body out, what's left of it.' He changed the subject. 'Anything fresh from you?'

'We've picked up another of the girl's customers. A chap called Purvis—Councillor Richard Purvis, he's managing director of Rootes Purvis Constructions. They've got their offices in that bloody great cube of concrete in the city centre.'

'How did you get on to him?'

'I took a chance and had a friendly word with Harkness. He's the chap who likes to be done up in leather straps so I just asked him how he managed about the buckles. You should have seen him. He went green. He's Daddy all right; he admits to visiting the flat every Wednesday evening.'

'What about last Wednesday?'

'He says the chick called him at his office and put him off. He's scared stiff that his wife is going to get wind of his adventures and he's willing to do the dirt on anybody. Purvis put him on to the girl in the first place.'

'Do you believe him when he says that

he was not at the flat on Wednesday evening?'

Gill shrugged. 'He hasn't got the guts to step on a worm.'

'What about Purvis?'

Gill gestured broadly. 'I had a word. A different proposition altogether. He doesn't scare. He's already threatening to complain to his friend, Mr Bellings. Can't have snotty nosed coppers flat footing into his private affairs.'

'What sort of chap is he?'

'He started as a builder's labourer and he's proud of it—says he's still got dirt under his fingernails to prove it. You wouldn't notice, I'd say his backside fitted the boss's chair very well.'

'No Mrs Purvis?'

Gill's hands sketched something small and fragile. 'A little grey cooing dove. They live in a bloody great house in Conniston Gardens, near where the Powells used to live. She married Purvis when he had his foot on the bottom rung and, by all accounts, she would have been happier if he'd stayed there.'

Wycliffe sighed. 'Everywhere you turn in this case you come across property— buying, selling, surveying, building.'

Gill flicked ash on the carpet. 'I reckon our Chris was working a nice little racket; but, somehow, I can't believe that was why she got clobbered.'

Wycliffe cut short another exposition and Gill got up to go. 'I think I'll have another go at Salt, even if he isn't directly mixed up in all this there's not much goes on under the counter that he doesn't know about.'

Wycliffe got out a bulky file and settled down to work. He was drawing up a report for the chief constable on the re-organization of the whole CID in the police area. Re-organization, as well as being addictive, attracts favourable notice in the press and in committees. No administrator worth his salt will allow the dust to settle on one totally unnecessary and time-consuming general post before starting another. Wycliffe had set himself the difficult task of proposing seemingly revolutionary changes which would, in fact, alter very little. This he hoped to achieve by the simple expedient of changing the names of offices and procedures without changing the work of the people concerned. He worked for half an hour before boredom got the better of him. His office oppressed him, he felt deadened by it, muted. Even if he stamped his foot the carpet absorbed the sound. Double glazing shut out the real world including the friendly and capricious draughts which had been such a feature of his old office. He lit his pipe and sat back in his chair.

Morris.

Whatever one thought of Gill's flights of fancy there could be no doubt that Morris had become a central figure in the case. Either it was his body which lay under the ruins in Middle Street or... Or what? He had given instructions for the boy's movements to be traced but he needed to know more about him. By all accounts his mother lived in a grey world on the fringe of reality and Morris had built his life round his work and round his painting; he seemed to spend most of his free time at the Old Custom House.

Wycliffe pressed a button on his intercom. 'Miss Saxton? I'm going out.' He knew that the poor girl had been waiting patiently for him to call her in with the post. Why did it give him a perverse satisfaction to frustrate her?

He drove to the same spot at the top of the cobbled alley and parked on a meter. The harbour and the waterfront still basked in sunshine, an enclave of peace surrounded and all but engulfed by the sprawling bustling city. The car park in front of the Old Custom House was empty. Why had he not parked there? He would have had difficulty in explaining. Perhaps he wanted to make his contribution to keeping the place apart. It was a place where one should walk.

The bookshop had not changed either, the same notice hung inside the glass door, Back Shortly. Last time Jarvis had been lunching at a restaurant in Bear Street. It was now a quarter to twelve, perhaps he started early and finished late.

The houses in Bear Street were early 19th-century town cottages, a row each side, their front doors opening off the street. A few of them had been converted into shops but most were still lived in. The restaurant was immediately behind the Old Custom House. There was a shop window through which he could see old fashioned marble-topped tables, a counter with an *espresso* machine and, behind the counter, an auburn haired girl. On an impulse he went in, the door bell pinged.

'Could I have a black coffee, please?'

A cheerful girl, freckled, with a large, generous mouth and a broad, flattish nose. She was refilling plastic salt pots.

'Quiet, isn't it?'

'It always is until we start serving lunches at one o'clock, then it's busy enough for an hour or so.' She was Irish.

He sat at a table near the counter and she brought him his coffee. A man in a chef's apron, red faced and stocky, stood for a moment in a doorway at the back of the shop then withdrew.

'I was looking for Mr Jarvis from the bookshop.'

'He doesn't come in until one.'

'The shop is shut.'

She grinned. 'He always goes for a walk before lunch if the weather is fine, his constitutional, he calls it.'

'What about Mr Robson?'

'What about him?'

'Does he have his lunch here?'

'Sometimes, it depends how he feels.' She went back to replenishing the salt pots.

'Two bachelors living alone, I don't suppose they do a lot of cooking.'

'None, as far as I know. We don't open in the evening but Dad cooks for them when he cooks for us and I take it in.'

'Take it in?'

'Through the back.' She indicated the back premises with a vague gesture. 'Our back opens into their yard.' She continued for a while, filling her salt pots. 'You're asking a lot of questions.'

'Do you know Paul Morris?'

'I know him, he spends a lot of time next door; what about him?' She wrinkled her forehead in a frown.

'Are you from the police? Is it about the girl who was murdered?'

He had really captured her attention now. 'You knew her?'

'Of course I knew her, she used to come next door. I didn't know what she was then, but it wouldn't have been difficult to guess.'

He had finished his coffee, now he paid for it and left. She came with him to the door. 'You don't think Paul Morris did it, do you?'

'I may come back to talk to you again.' Despite the frank, open manner he had the uncomfortable impression that she was acting a part for his benefit. The Irish are born actors. The trouble is, if you are a policeman long enough you come to suspect innocence itself.

Jarvis was back, standing in his shop doorway, presumably waiting for one o'clock. 'My dear boy. Another visit?' He did not sound pleased.

'I want to talk to Mr Robson.'

'To Derek? I'm afraid he's not here. He's a young man with a life of his own and business is slack just now. It seemed a good chance for him to have a few days off.'

'Where has he gone?'

Jarvis looked pained by the lack of good manners. 'I didn't ask him, dear boy. I imagine that he wanted to spend Christmas with friends, but I have no idea where.'

'I would like to see the studio where Morris paints if you have no objection.'

'Objection? Why should I object?' But it was obvious that he was not happy.

A wide passage lit by a large skylight led off the shop and it was here that Jarvis displayed paintings by favoured members of the Arts Society. They showed a range of talent from laboured picture-postcard scenes to self-confident landscapes and portraits. There were two doors off the corridor, both open. One led into the kitchen, tall and narrow and gloomy, the other into a sitting-room full of dusty furniture which was, obviously, scarcely ever used. But a french window opened on to a courtyard dominated by a magnificent cedar. At the end of the passage, stairs led up to the first floor and the smells of glue and mouldering paper began to blend with the odour of oil-paint and turpentine. Neither the stairs nor the first floor passage had any floor covering and the planks were worn unevenly. Narrower, twisting stairs continued up to the attics.

'Derek has his rooms on this floor, would you like to see?'

Wycliffe wondered why he was being given the chance.

In contrast to the ground floor the passage was brilliantly lit by the sun flooding through windows along its entire length. They were evidently in the part of the building which was built out on the pillars; the tall windows looked down on the empty square and, beyond, to the harbour which seemed incredibly blue in the winter sunshine.

'Bedroom.' Jarvis opened a door briefly, disclosing a small room with a single bed, neat and tidy but otherwise unremarkable. Was Jarvis using the occasion to show that his relationship with his assistant was respectable? 'And this is his sitting-room.'

A large, comfortable-looking room with a monster settee or divan and a couple of reasonable looking armchairs upholstered in pale brown leather. The window overlooked the courtyard and the cedar tree. Over the mantelpiece there was a framed, obvious self-portrait of Christine Powell, a head and shoulders. It seemed to Wycliffe cruelly satirical. Painted in different shades of green on an olive-green background, the face emerged, lime green with near white highlights. The eyes had been cleverly elongated and slanted to make them sinister yet they were still the eyes of the photograph Smith had taken and they seemed to follow Wycliffe disturbingly as he moved about the room.

Jarvis saw his interest. 'That's the sort of girl she was.'

'She gave the painting to Robson?'

'She painted it for him.'

Wycliffe realized that he was being told something. Having failed to get rid of him Jarvis was giving him information.

'She came pretty often with Paul, then,

latterly, she came on her own.'

'To see Robson?'

Jarvis smiled. 'Not to see me, dear boy. She was a trollop and Paul is an innocent. Derek isn't above taking advantage of a situation like that; in fact, I sometimes think he has a cruel streak in his nature.'

'Does Morris know?'

Jarvis pursed his lips. 'I doubt if Derek advertised the fact, but it would have been quite in character for the girl to tell him herself.'

'I assume Morris and Robson were not on good terms?'

'On the contrary, dear boy, they are the best of friends. Derek has charm and sophistication which Paul sadly lacks and I am quite sure that the boy admires and envies him.'

Wycliffe walked over to the window and stood looking down in to the courtyard. Beyond the cedar someone had parked a red E-type and beyond that there was a black van with lettering on the side which he could not read. 'Is that your car?'

'Derek's.'

'There must be money in the book business.'

Jarvis answered stiffly. 'We do well enough.'

'What exactly does Robson do, Mr Jarvis?'

'He's our buyer, that's his main job.'

'Buyer?'

Jarvis was straightening the cushions on the settee. 'We sell books of antiquarian interest and importance, these books have to be bought, dear boy. You can't just put in an order for ten gross assorted.'

'How do you set about it?'

'We specialize in foreign books, mainly French. Three or four times a year Derek takes the van across on the ferry and makes the rounds of the French dealers. We have a connection, built up over the years. Before Derek came I did the buying myself.'

'So Derek buys the books and brings them over in the van?'

'Yes.' Jarvis looked puzzled, wondering what the chief superintendent was getting at. Wycliffe did not know himself. 'Derek also travels in this country, buying from dealers and attending sales.'

'I suppose you sell mainly to collectors?'

'Collectors, museums, libraries, universities—we have every sort of customer.'

Wycliffe took out his pipe. 'May I?'

Jarvis made an expansive gesture. 'Liberty Hall, dear boy.'

Wycliffe was undergoing an experience which he had known many times before. In the course of an investigation, after a seemingly endless series of interrogations, interviews and reports, when his ideas were confused and contradictory, his mind would suddenly clear and the salient facts would stand out in sharp relief as though a lens had suddenly brought them into proper focus. At this stage he would not necessarily distinguish any pattern in the facts but he would, from then on, be able to classify and relate them so that a pattern would eventually emerge. Oddly enough this usually happened to him when he was talking, as now, at random—'fishing'. And he had just learned at least one new fact; the association between the dead girl and Derek Robson could have made two people intensely, perhaps dangerously jealous. Andrew Jarvis who almost certainly had more than a professional interest in his assistant, and Paul Morris who seemed to have discovered the agonies of calf love at twenty-eight.

Wycliffe's eyes kept coming back to the

portrait over the mantelpiece. Will the real Christine Powell, please stand up? Experience had taught him that things were never that simple. Even the most uncomplicated human beings do not fit into pigeon holes, and Christine Powell had been tantalizingly complex. Whore, business woman, probably blackmailer, Sunday painter. She might have been all these and more and it would probably be wrong to think of one label as being truer than another. If the painting were evidence, her estimate of herself was anything but flattering.

'I would like to see the studio.'

'Of course.'

The stairs were narrow, twisted and steep. The passage at the top was lit only by a small and dirty skylight. There were three attics, two small and one much larger. One of the small rooms was Jarvis's bindery. There was a bench with the tools of the trade and a number of old books in different stages of restoration from sewn sections to the all but finished article with its leather binding and gilded spine. Jarvis displayed his work with pride. 'It's a hobby more than anything else, I enjoy working with my hands.'

The second of the small rooms was a book store with slatted shelves round the walls and the books laid out in batches. 'Our last consignment,' Jarvis said, 'we haven't had a chance to sort them yet.'

The studio was large, lit by two dormer windows and, like the other attics, it was open to the roof trusses. There were shelves occupying the whole of both end walls and these were laden with large books and portfolios. An old fashioned slow-combustion stove stood in the centre of the room and its iron smoke pipe disappeared through the roof. A red mica window glowed pleasantly and waves of gentle warmth radiated in all directions.

'I try to keep the room warm and well ventilated to avoid mildew, dear boy.' He waved his hand in the direction of the bookshelves. 'I collect prints and illustrated books, some of them are quite valuable.'

There was a large easel near one of the windows, its back to Wycliffe, and a table with a palette, a jar of brushes and tubes of oil-paint.

'That's where he works.'

Wycliffe was pleased with the room, it was just such a room as he would have liked himself, but what would he do in it?

As always when entering a room for the first time he was drawn to the window. Through the branches of the cedar which topped the building he could look down into the backyards of the little houses in Bear Street where women were hanging out their washing, taking advantage of the sun.

'Do you mind if I look round?'

Jarvis shrugged with unassumed indifference. 'Help yourself, dear boy.'

If he had stopped to think Wycliffe might have asked himself why he was showing such an interest in the place and he would have had difficulty in finding an answer. He had what amounted to a superstition about coincidences and there were certainly coincidences connected with the Old Custom House. It was a key property in Powell's development scheme and his sister had held him to ransom for it; it was also the place where Paul Morris had spent most of his free time, some of it with the dead girl. Finally it was where he had claimed to be when she was murdered.

Wycliffe wandered round the room with apparent aimlessness. He looked at everything. The large portfolios were labelled with the names of famous wood engravers and print makers, including a few Japanese. The books were arranged according to the illustrator and not the author. In another section there were books on the techniques of wood engraving and of print making. At last Wycliffe reached the easel and stood looking at the picture which, presumably, Morris had worked at on the night of the murder. It seemed complete, a large painting, over four feet high. Jarvis joined him.

'What do you think of that?'

The painting was a view of the city centre as it might appear from a low flying helicopter. The effect was remarkable, partly because the picture lacked any consistent perspective; each building seemed to have been drawn from a unique point of view but its architecture, though simplified, had not been distorted. Through the apposition of several such images the picture achieved an effect of controlled craziness. And the colours helped, flat and innocent of gradation, they presented a faceted whole which had a restrained gaiety.

'What do you think of it?' Jarvis repeated.

Wycliffe, who found it impossible to lie about such things, said, 'I don't know.'

Jarvis was clearly disappointed. 'But, my dear boy, anyone could see with half an eye that there is talent there, quite exceptional talent.'

Wycliffe was affable. 'I expect you are right, but to me there was more obvious talent in the self-portrait downstairs.'

But Jarvis scouted the idea. 'Exhibitionism, dear boy. All of a piece with the rest of her. I won't deny that she had a certain technique but...' He went over to a stack of canvases placed against the wall and selected one which he placed on the easel. It was a head and shoulders portrait of a young man. 'That's another of hers, a portrait of Paul, and bloody cruel it is. The silly boy brought it here to show me.'

Wycliffe had not met Paul Morris but he could believe that the portrait was less than charitable. The lantern jaw, the prominent adam's apple, the solemn, dark eyes exaggerated by the lenses of powerful spectacles, the uncertain expression of the thin lips and the black hair fitting like a priest's skull-cap. Wycliffe had the impression of brittle strength.

'There's more in that picture of her than of him and that's not what painting is about. This is pure self-indulgence...' Jarvis was on a hobby horse and Wycliffe had no desire to listen to a dissertation on the integrity of art. He continued to prowl while Jarvis talked.

There were two drawers in the little painting table but they held nothing of interest. Charcoal sticks, pencils, rubbers, a couple of palette knives and a sketch book with nothing in it. What had he hoped or expected to find?'

There were two long grey linen coats hanging on a hook near the easel, one was covered with paint stains. 'Do these belong to Morris?'

'The paint stained one, the other is mine.'

Wycliffe lifted the jacket down and felt in the pockets. Jarvis watched him, frowning. 'You really do suspect the boy?'

Wycliffe was laying out the contents of the pockets on the table. A handkerchief, a pencil, a 'Bic', a soda-mint and a screwed up paper tissue. From the other pocket he removed a piece of white chalk and three envelopes. The envelopes were all addressed to Morris, one at his office, the others at the Old Custom House.

'He has post sent here?'

'Sometimes. He buys his paints and canvas from a London firm and that comes here.'

The envelope addressed to Morris's office was empty but it had evidently been used as a memo for there was a list of colours scribbled on the back. The second envelope contained an invoice for canvas but it was the contents of the third envelope which seemed to put a new complexion on the whole case. Morris's name and the Old Custom House address had been printed neatly on the envelope and inside, written in the same manner, was a short note unsigned:

YOUR GIRL FRIEND IS A WHORE. IF YOU DON'T BELIEVE ME YOU CAN FIND OUT FOR YOURSELF ANY EVENING 9 STANLEY STREET. BOTTOM FLAT.

Wycliffe held the note for Jarvis to read. 'You must see whatever comes here for Morris?'

Jarvis fiddled with the silver curls at his

temples. 'Not always, sometimes Derek takes in the post.'

'This seems to have come by hand, you don't remember this particular envelope?'

'No, dear boy, I don't.'

'What do you do with post which comes for him?'

'One of us would put it on his table here.'

'So that this might have been waiting for him when he arrived here on Wednesday evening?'

'It's quite possible, dear boy.' Jarvis seemed upset. 'I suppose you see this as giving him a stronger motive?'

'May I use your telephone?'

'What? Of course, dear boy. Downstairs in my office.'

'I'm taking this jacket and the contents, I'll give you a receipt.'

He telephoned his headquarters from Jarvis's office and gave instructions for Paul Morris's description to be circulated. '...to be brought in for questioning in connection with the murder of Christine Powell.'

Jarvis was standing at his elbow, he seemed to find it difficult to believe what was happening. The day before, when asked if he thought Morris might be guilty, he had said, 'It's possible.' But that was talk, this was real. 'I can't believe that the boy...'

CHAPTER SIX

Number three Lavington Place is one of a terrace of Regency houses with ornate, cast-iron verandahs on the first floor. The terrace had been given the Civic Trust treatment with icing pink stucco and white windows and doors. Even if Salt had no taste himself he had allowed the experts to have their way. Gill was received in the drawing-room where the Civic Trust had not penetrated and the Salts had gone a little off the rails with a huge, chromium plated gas fire, 'antique dogs', and wall-to-wall carpeting which created spots before the eyes. Mrs Salt, a little brown mouse of a woman, smiled and looked glad to see him.

'You're lucky to catch us in, Mr Gill, we've just come back from doing our Christmas shopping, haven't we, Martin?'

'Whisky, Mr Gill? Or is it too early?' Salt went across to a miniature bar. 'Would you rather Mavis stayed or went, it's all the same to us, isn't it, Mavis?'

Mrs Salt agreed.

Gill was smooth. 'I suppose as it's a question of ownership of property, it's Mrs Salt I should talk to.' He grinned like a cannibal presented with a tender missionary. 'But I've no doubt that you are in her confidence.'

Mrs Salt got up and went but she cast a slightly nervous glance at her husband as she turned to shut the door.

'This is good whisky.'

'It should be, the price I pay for it.'

Gill was making himself comfortable in an armchair upholstered in cherry coloured velvet. 'I'll stop arsing about and come to the point. It seems more than likely that Christine Powell died intestate so that her little lot should go to big brother Jonathan.' He chuckled. 'I may as well admit that I rather fancy the idea of him coming into a thriving little business in prostitution. But it means, if only for the look of the thing, he'll fall over backwards to be helpful to us. His lawyers will dissect the estate and offer each little bit for inspection under the microscope before getting shot of it.' Gill leered at Salt. 'You get my point?'

Salt stared at the glass in his hand. 'I don't doubt you're right, Mr Gill, but I can't see what it's got to do with me.'

'No? Everything will come out—everything, including the building in Bear Street which Powell will inherit from his sister. Don't tell me you haven't had a finger in that pie.'

Salt took time to consider. His moustache glistened with droplets of whisky which he had been too preoccupied to wipe off. 'There's really no secret about that, Mr Gill. The place belonged to me—to Mavis that is, long before I had that little spot of bother with the law. I bought it off a chap called Fitzy Simmonds who conned me into it. I was young then and Fitzy could have flogged Buck House to the Duke. I had some crazy idea of doing a conversion job—flats—down-town pads for young executives, that sort of crap. It was only after, I realized that young executives don't have any money. In any case you couldn't convert that barracks into a mausoleum.' He smiled disarmingly. 'I've learnt a lot since them days, Mr Gill.'

Gill was unimpressed. 'Too much. Now cut the biography and get on with it.'

'Well, to cut a long story short, I rented the place on a lease to Andrew Jarvis and that lease falls in in two years.'

'Where did the Powell girl come in?' Gill put down his glass, took a packet of cheroots from his pocket and lit one.

Salt thought while a gilded clock, let into a mirror over the mantelpiece, ticked fifteen seconds away. Then he ran his fingers through his thin sandy hair. 'I hope this is all off the record, Mr Gill?'

'I don't see anybody with a notebook, do you?'

'Not that I've anything to hide. As I told you, I used to go to Chris for—'

Gill raised an enormous hand. 'So it's Chris now, is it? Yesterday you thought her name was Lily and you were bowled over by the news that she was George Powell's daughter.'

Salt spread his hands expansively. 'Well, Mr Gill, that's understandable, isn't it? I mean, when a man's got form, like me, it don't pay to know too much too soon.'

'Your trouble is more likely to be knowing too much too late, Salt.'

'Well, as I was saying, I went to Chris for a bit off the ration. She was quite a girl and not only for what you might think, she had a head on her, a good business head.'

'You should know.'

'I do know, Mr Gill. We saw eye to eye about a lot of things. Anyway, one evening about six months ago she asked me if I wanted to sell the Old Custom House. I said I would consider a proposition and nothing more was said then. A day or two later she spoke to me on the blower and asked me how long Jarvis's lease had to run. I told her two years and then she made me an offer—a very good offer. After a bit of haggling for form's sake we made a deal.'

'You knew why she wanted the place?'

Salt grinned, almost with affection. 'She didn't give much away but I had a shrewd suspicion.'

'And you mean to say you parted with the place without trying to screw Powell yourself?'

Salt looked smug. 'I reckon I owed her, Mr Gill.'

'Since when has a thing like that bothered you? What did she have on you, Salt?'

'Nothing, Mr Gill! Nothing, as God's my witness!'

Gill relaxed, glancing round the room and studying the furniture. 'Somebody did you a good turn last night, Salt.'

'Me? That don't happen very often, Mr Gill, what was it?'

'Somebody set alight to twenty-four Middle Street, the office of the City Property Trust.'

Salt shook his head. 'I heard about it this morning but it don't affect me, Mr Gill. I remember Mr Wycliffe asked me about the Trust.'

'He did. Now I'm asking you and if I were you I'd do some remembering. You were hand-in-glove with the dead girl, you sold her the reversion of the lease on the Old Custom House, so don't tell me it comes as a surprise to you that she *was* the City Property Trust.'

Salt poured himself another whisky without asking Gill to join him. 'I'd like to know why you're pushing me so hard, Mr Gill.'

'Because you're a crook and because you served about a fifth of the time you should have served if there was any justice in this world. Now, what about this City Property Trust?'

Salt sipped his whisky before replying. 'Well, it's true she did some of her business in the name of this Trust—'

'Did you ever go to Middle Street?'

'A couple of times, three or four maybe.'

'Last night?'

'I swear—'

'Don't bother. She lived in the Middle Street flat, didn't she?'

'She seemed to spend a fair bit of time there—most nights, I think.'

'So if she had the dirt on somebody that's where she would keep it?'

Salt shook his head vigorously. 'I don't know anything about that, Mr Gill. All I know, she had nothing on me.'

Gill lit another of his cheroots. 'Going back to the property you sold her, was the sale completed?'

'Three weeks ago.'

'So what happens now?'

Salt frowned. 'Search me, Mr Gill. All I can say is, brotherly love apart, things seem to have turned out pretty well for Powell.' There was a moment of silence then he added, hopefully, 'Satisfied, Mr Gill?'

'No, but I'll look into it.'

Salt was peevish. 'What I've told you is straight up and you can see for yourself I had no reason to do her in. Anyway, I was soft on her.'

'Did she ever tell you anything about

herself? Anything which might suggest somebody was putting the frighteners on her?'

Salt looked serious. 'No, she never talked much about herself anyway. It was only after we started doing a bit of business together that I found out who she was.'

'You've no ideas, then?'

'No, Mr Gill, I wish I had. Of course, she wasn't exactly what you'd call a good insurance risk, the way she went on.'

Gill was half inclined to believe him. 'One more question, this Jarvis chap, what's his racket?'

'Has he got one?'

'I'm asking.'

Salt shook his head. 'As far as I know he buys and sells books.'

Gill stood up. 'That's all for the moment, but be around, I'm sure we shall need you.'

At the door Gill stopped to look at a garish oil-painting of a nude girl seen through a gauze veil. 'Pretty.'

'That's a genuine oil-painting, Mr Gill, none of your reproduction rubbish. I paid good money for that and I'll give it you if I don't lose out over all this.'

Mrs Salt came out to see him off,

treating him as though he had been a welcome guest. 'A happy Christmas, Mr Gill.'

As he drove back to headquarters Gill thought things over. The odds were that Salt had told him the truth. Only one nagging doubt remained. It was conceivable that Salt had seen, or thought he had seen, a chance to get his hands in the Powell till. And if that had somehow gone wrong...

Wycliffe did not feel at home anywhere until he had established a routine. When a case took him to a new area for a while he would try to give his days some sort of pattern, even if it amounted to no more than having a drink in the same bar at about the same time or buying a paper at the same shop. The recent transfer of his headquarters had wiped the slate clean and he was in the process of sketching a new design. His lunch routine had been settled from the first day. By chance he had found Teague's eating house and from the moment he had entered the place he knew that he was destined to eat a great many meals there.

Teague's was wedged between a supermarket and a bank, its frontage was small but it ran back, little more than a passage, for fifty yards or more. There were two lines of old fashioned booths with a matted walk between. Each booth accommodated two people and there was a hook on which to hang hats and coats. The table was covered with a white damask cloth and there was a plated cruet stand with glass bottles. It was not cheap and there was a set meal each day, but the quality of the food and its preparation ensured that there were few empty booths.

Wycliffe took Gill to lunch there.

'Cosy.'

The set meal was soup or tomato juice followed by roast beef with a choice of vegetables and topped off by a soufflé.

'Drink?'

'Beer.'

'They do a very good lager here which I haven't come across anywhere else.'

It came, pale gold with a delicate lacy foam and nicely chilled. Gill took a gulp and said nothing.

'Like it?'

Gill shrugged. 'Give me a draught bitter any day.'

The main course arrived.

Wycliffe told Gill of the anonymous note

he had found in the pocket of Morris's painting coat. 'As you so elegantly put it, "the dirt from Stanley Street in a plain wrapper".'

Gill smiled. 'I told you.'

Wycliffe helped himself to horseradish. 'I've put out a call for Morris and I've sent the note to forensic.' He spoke almost defensively. 'We shall look silly if it turns out to be his body in the fire.'

Gill looked at him curiously. 'I don't see why; it wouldn't mean that he hadn't killed the girl.' Gill was a master of the double negative. He patted his lips with his table napkin. 'I know what's bothering you even if Morris did kill the girl, why would he want to start that particular bonfire? It would have been more logical, more understandable, at least, if it had been the place in Stanley Street. Obliterate the scene of her degradation and all that crap. Sow it with salt. I agree, but there are plenty of others who might feel relieved to hear that the Middle Street flat had gone up in smoke taking their dirty little secrets with it. Any one of them might have decided to go in for a spot of arson.'

'And the body?'

'One thing at a time. We shall know

more when Franks is able to take a look.'
An onlooker might have suspected that Gill
was trying to be reassuring. He changed
the subject: across the gangway a waitress
was bending over one of the tables making
out a bill and showing a neat little behind
sheathed in black tights.

'I've often wondered why brunettes have
more shapely backsides than blondes...'

They had decided against the soufflé and
ordered coffee. The regulars seemed much
at home; after their meal they lingered to
do *The Times* or the *Telegraph* crossword,
some even played chess with travellers'
chess sets, resuming a game where it had
been broken off the day before. Wycliffe
looked round with satisfaction.

After lunch he did not go back to his
office. As Gill had seen, he was restless and
ill-at-ease because he could not formulate
in his mind any coherent view of the case.
He was floundering. He could not believe
that Christine Powell had been murdered
because of her shady deals in property,
he did not believe either that she had
died because she was blackmailing her
customers. There was no proof that she
had blackmailed anybody but, even if she
had, the victims of blackmail rarely turn

to murder. Had Morris killed the girl in a frenzy of disillusionment and anger? As Gill had said, it was plausible but the sequel, if sequel it proved to be, was not. The fire in Middle Street did not fit.

He was walking through the city centre, jostled by men and girls returning to offices and shops after the lunchtime break. A surprising number of them were carrying bottles for office parties after work. A news-vendor's bill caught his eye. It had two captions:

POWELL MURDER
BROTHER AT POLICE HQ

and

BODY IN CITY BLAZE
FOUL PLAY SUSPECTED.

Evidently the press had not seen any connection but later editions would almost certainly carry the news that the City Property Trust and Christine Powell were one and the same. The scope for journalistic speculation would spoil Mr Bellings's Christmas.

He was walking up Middle Street where

a fire tender was still parked. The smell of charred timber was overpowering. A section of the temporary screen had been removed and a lorry had backed over the pavement to begin the removal of the rubbish. A constable, there to ward off sightseers, saluted. He had nothing to do, for the dust and the urgency of Christmas shopping were keeping people away.

Wycliffe was surprised at the transformation which had been achieved in a short time. The back part of the building had been shored up with a net-work of steel tubes and there was a ladder up to the first floor. The mass of rubble had been reduced and, unless the two firemen had been seeing visions, the uncovering of the body must be imminent. Five or six men, wearing heat-proof gloves and boots, were working under the joint supervision of Sergeant Scales, and the young fire officer Wycliffe had seen in the morning. Sergeant Smith, the photographer, was standing apart, morose as usual, his hands thrust deep into the pockets of his overcoat. He acknowledged Wycliffe with a barely perceptible nod.

'The rubble is being taken to a tip, sir, but the rest—everything that looks like anything—is being taken to an empty garage at headquarters.'

Wycliffe chatted for a moment then asked if it was safe to go up to the first floor. The fire officer was cautious. 'It's not safe, sir, the roof is very dodgy and the joists in the passage are not much more than charcoal, but if you're careful...'

Wycliffe picked his way over the rubble and climbed the ladder. He could have gone round the back and up the iron staircase but that would have brought him to the kitchen and he would still have had to make the difficult traverse to the bedroom where he wanted to go.

There had been a passage running parallel with the street, between the front and back rooms. The wall of this passage nearest the street had largely disintegrated, pulverized by the heat, but the further wall was still intact though stripped of plaster and badly cracked.

'Look out for those joists, sir,' the nervous young fireman called to him. The floor of the passage had gone and the joists were partially carbonized but it was not too difficult to step across into the doorway of the room in which he had glimpsed a bed when he had reconnoitred the previous evening. The room was a remarkable sight, he was reminded of the freak effects he had seen during the blitz. The back wall of the house seemed undisturbed except where the window had been demolished by the firemen. Even the blue, brocade curtains were still hanging. To the left of the window there was a large wardrobe, ivory white with gilt fittings, to the right, the pale blue textured wallpaper seemed undamaged.

The bed, against the wall at right angles to the window, had been pushed aside but the bed-head lamp and the picture above were still in place. The bed and the blue carpet were sodden with water and soot had been trodden in, but the only fire damage was on the wall against the passage where the plaster had crumbled, exposing the brickwork, and the carpet was scorched in a broad band. Apart from the bed and the wardrobe there was a dressing-table with a cracked mirror which hung drunkenly in its clips.

He was intrigued by the picture over the bed which was, obviously, another Paul Morris. This time his unique vision had been directed at the docks. Interest was created by soaring cranes, gantries and masts, squat warehouses and intersecting railway lines, each royally indifferent to its neighbour in the matter of perspective but contriving, none the less to achieve a unity which defied analysis.

So, whatever she thought of Morris, she had thought enough of his work to hang a picture over her bed.

He opened the wardrobe, expecting it to be crammed with clothes but there were relatively few. A couple of winter coats, half-a-dozen dresses, some blouses and three or four skirts, a couple of pairs of slacks and an anorak. There were two handbags on a shelf and a rack of shoes including a pair of heavy walking shoes. He knew little about women's clothes but he thought that these might be described as 'quiet', almost dowdy. The unlikely adjective 'demure' occurred to him—for the wardrobe of a tart.

He went through the handbags and through the pockets of all the garments which had pockets but his haul was unimpressive. One item only seemed to link her with Morris, a ticket for a concert by the Bournemouth Symphony Orchestra in the Central Hall. Clipped to it was a slip of paper on which was written in faultless italic script, 'I hope you can use this. All my love, P.' The ticket had been for the previous evening.

The dressing-table, which incorporated a set of drawers, told him little. She had been restrained in her use of make-up and her underclothes were plain and unglamorous like those he had seen in the Stanley Street flat. It was difficult to imagine the girl who had worn them using her body to trap men. There remained the little bed-side unit which consisted of a small cupboard with a couple of shelves and a drawer. The cupboard was empty except for a box of paper tissues while the drawer contained two books and a bottle of sleeping tablets. One of the books, well thumbed, was a translation of the *Journal of Marie Bashkirsteff* and the other was a paper-backed edition of Anthony Storr's *Human Aggression*.

There was a noise of someone scrambling over the joists and Sergeant Scales came in. The best dressed man in the squad, he was examining his overcoat to see if he had picked up any soot on the way.

'They've uncovered the body, sir. Not enough to move it yet but they won't be long. At the moment Sergeant Smith is taking photographs.'

'Have you told Franks?'

'I've sent a message through the duty room, sir, and I've asked them to send the van.'

Scales was looking round with interest. 'She seems to have had good taste. From the bits we've found and this, it looks as though she had a nice flat.' Scales was an authority on flats; his wife was a university lecturer and the two of them lived a Box-and Cox life in a very elegant flat on the outskirts of the city. 'I like the picture...'

For the next forty minutes Wycliffe stood watching while the men worked to free the body and at each stage of the process Sergeant Smith took photographs. By a fortunate chance two beams had fallen across one another and helped to keep the weight of the rubble clear of the body, which, otherwise, must have been crushed. But the beams were several feet long so that removing them was a slow business. After a little while Franks arrived and they stood together in silence, watching. In another hour it would be dark but the work of clearing the site would continue under flood lights already rigged from neighbouring buildings.

It is notoriously difficult to predict what fire will do to a human body and how long it will take to do it. A great deal depends on the clothing, on the flammability of neighbouring objects and, of course, on the temperature attained. In this case the body was a blackened mass with calcined bone showing over part of the skull and at the knees; vestiges of shoes remained on the feet.

Franks looked at the body with distaste. 'I hate burnings, I always have.'

When they had got a sheet under the body and started to lift it Wycliffe left. He was driven back to headquarters in a Panda car. It was almost dark, the street lamps were on and the shop windows blazed with light. The air was clear and crisp so that everything seemed miraculously sharp and clean. People were out window shopping. Multi-coloured neon stars were suspended at intervals over the main shopping streets and snatches of carols churned out by loudspeakers reached him as his driver snaked through the traffic. 'Peace on earth and mercy mild. God and sinners reconciled.' But not yet.

WPC Saxton was hammering away at her

typewriter. The bronze chrysanthemums were looking as fresh as ever.

After he had glanced at the additions to his 'In' tray he walked down the corridor to a room at the back of the building where Sergeant Bourne, surrounded by paper and filing cabinets, looked after collation and did whatever other jobs came his way. Bourne was twenty-six, a graduate, sharp of feature and of mind. Up and coming. He had a thick, dark moustache very slightly turned down at the ends, modern without being trendy.

Wycliffe walked to the window and stood looking out. Bourne's room overlooked the headquarters car park, now lit up. Beyond, unseen in the darkness, trees and fields stretched away to the horizon needing only outline planning permission to turn them into a developer's paradise.

'Can I help you, sir?'

Wycliffe glanced round the room which seemed bare and bright, a place to work. 'Nice room you've got here.'

'Sir?'

'I said you've got a nice room.'

Bourne was cautious. 'Quite nice, sir.'

'No carpet.' Wycliffe stamped his foot on the linoleum.

Bourne frowned. 'No, no carpet, sir.' He was worried, you never knew when you were being tested, or why.

'You are a graduate in English?'

Bourne brightened. 'Yes, sir. Had I known that I would enter the police I would have studied Law.'

'Are you on good terms with the City Librarian?'

'I know him, sir.'

'Do you also know Andrew Jarvis at the Old Custom House?'

'The bookseller—yes, indeed, sir.'

'Good! I've got a job for you. I want you to find out what you can about Jarvis's standing as a dealer. I understand that he specializes in foreign antiquarian books, mainly French. What sort of reputation does he have and what sort of business does he do?'

Bourne would have spoken but Wycliffe stopped him. 'At the same time, see what you can find out about Jarvis as a man. He seems to be a collector on his own account—prints and illustrated books. How well is he known? What does he spend?'

'I doubt if the City Librarian will—'

'So do I, but he should be able to put you on to the right people. Use your

180

initiative but be discreet.'

Bourne glanced at the papers on his table. 'I've got one or two things—'

'They can wait.'

'If you say so, sir.'

'And Bourne—'

'Sir?' The brown eyes were anxious to please but cautious.

'Never mind.' If chief constables had batons there would be one in Bourne's haversack. What need had he also of good advice?

Back in his office Wycliffe dictated a memo to CRO asking for any information they might have on Andrew Jarvis and Derek Robson.

CHAPTER SEVEN

Wycliffe felt heavy and depressed. The body he had seen, charred and unrecognizable, had almost certainly been alive twenty-four hours earlier. On his way home the previous night he had reconnoitred the Middle Street premises and felt uneasy, but he had postponed any investigation until the following day. Too late. His reason had been sound, he needed firmer evidence of the dead girl's connection with the premises; but it was possible that his caution had cost a man his life and it was certain that evidence which might have been obtained from the flat had now been destroyed.

A casual tap on the door and Jimmy Gill walked in.

'I thought you might like to be brought up to date on Bates, the estate agent.' Gill took his usual seat and lit the inevitable cheroot. 'Bates left home just after eleven this morning and went to his office where he stayed until one o'clock. Young Dixon was parked outside trying to look like a lamp post. About half past twelve Bates was joined by a chap called Ellis, a lawyer of Morley, Prisk and Ellis. I've made some enquiries and it seems that, despite the brass plate, Ellis is the sole member of the firm; he's been doing Bates's conveyancing for years and he's been responsible for the legal side of all the girl's deals which involved Bates. Bates and Ellis went out to lunch at the Plume of Feathers and, after lunch, our intrepid young detective followed them here.'

'Here?'

'Here. They asked to speak to you but settled for me. Bates obviously had the wind up and might have done something silly but Ellis had his head screwed on. "My client has done nothing illegal." He is a little chap, wizened like a monkey.' Gill's hand and features brought the words to startling life. 'He agrees that Bates and the girl operated as a team with the girl providing the brains. Bates has been buying and selling property for years but only since he got together with the girl about two years ago has he been making real money. Ellis admits that the girl had inside information on a number of deals, but he claims that there was no reason to think that it had been obtained illegally and, even if it had been, neither he nor his client had had any part in it.'

Gill sighed. 'A smooth bastard, twisted as a corkscrew, but I've no reason to think he was telling outright lies.'

'Did he tell you where his client spent last night?'

'Believe it or not, Bates has a fancy woman. She lives in a flat in Belle Vue. I found that much out before this pair of clowns arrived and I've seen the lady—all mouth and tit as you might expect; but it isn't every girl who will share her bed with a box of Kleenex.'

'He was with her all night?'

'That's his story and she confirms it.'

Gill had also had a report from the detective who had been given the job of tracing Morris's movements. Morris had left home the previous morning to go to work and had arrived there, as usual, just before nine o'clock. At the offices of Lloyd and Winter the staff had been questioned and Jane Williams, the plump blonde in the reception desk had tried to be helpful.

'He wasn't himself, I could see that the

minute he came through that door. Usually he was so polite, not like some of them. Always a pleasant "Good morning, Miss Williams" and a remark about the weather. He's a nice young man—not married and he supports his widowed mother...'

'How was he different yesterday morning?'

'Different? Oh, yes, well, he looked like a ghost and he just walked through here and up the stairs without a word. When I took him his coffee round eleven he was just sitting there—' She frowned. 'What's it all about? I mean, he's missing now, isn't he?'

'Do you operate the switchboard?'

'Except in my lunchtime when another girl does it.'

'Can you remember if Mr Morris received any phone calls yesterday?'

A brief silence while she thought. 'I was trying to remember; I know I put through one call but there could have been more. Most of the calls go to one of the senior partners. I know he had one call before lunch because he was a long time answering. Mr Winter was waiting for me to get a call for him and I was a bit flustered. Then, about the middle of the afternoon, he made a call, he asked me for a line. I offered to get the number for him but he said, "No, it's personal".'

'You didn't happen to overhear?'

'I don't listen in!'

Mr Lloyd, one of the senior partners, had not seen Morris all that day but Mr Winter had talked to him about a certain specification and thought that he was sickening for something. 'It seemed to me that he was coming down with 'flu. There's a lot of it about and I wasn't a bit surprised when he didn't turn up this morning.'

Morris had left the office at about six and vanished.

'At least we should be able to trace his car,' Wycliffe said. 'Keep them at it, Jimmy.'

When Gill had gone Wycliffe was about to settle down to read the accumulated reports when the telephone rang. 'Wycliffe.'

'Switchboard, sir. We have a woman on the line who insists on speaking to you personally. She says she has information about Christine Powell.'

'Put her through.' Some kink probably. All detectives should be anonymous, once your name appears in the press you become a sitting duck.

'Wycliffe.'

A girlish voice, creamy with the local brogue. She was matter-of-fact. 'I want to speak to you, I think I should have done it before but it's best not to know much when your chaps ask questions. All the same, I don't want him to get away with it.'

'Who?'

'The man who killed her, of course.'

'Who are you?'

Hesitation. 'I'm not coming down to the nick.'

That explained it. Somebody who had had more than one brush with the law—and a girl at that. 'Do you live in Stanley Street?'

Another pause. 'Make up your mind.'

'Yes.'

'Number fifteen?'

'How did you know?'

'Upper or lower flat?'

'Lower.'

One of the girls from the other house in Stanley Street which had belonged to Christine Powell. 'I'll come over.'

'Now?'

'I'll be there in twenty minutes.'

In Prince's Street he was held up behind

a convoy of lorries making for the docks but Stanley Street was deserted. Number fifteen, like number nine, had had a face lift. The orange front door was opened before he could ring the bell.

'Are you Lesley Birch?' He had looked her up in the reports before leaving the office.

'That's me, you'd best come in.'

She was plump, running to fat but still pretty. Fair hair, blue eyes and a pink and white complexion. She wore a loose fitting blue frock cut low so that it showed her heavy, sagging breasts. She gave the impression of slovenly opulence. The sort of girl men tell their troubles to. Mammary psychology. Her room too, was frayed and tatty with lots of grubby chintz. Wycliffe was not immune to the seductive appeal of controlled sluttishness. An invitation to unbutton, morally as well as physically.

He sat opposite her in one of the chintz covered armchairs. She was entirely relaxed, flopped in her chair. 'I knew her, you see, she was a friend...' She said it defensively as though he might doubt her word. 'She used to drop in two or three times a week when she wanted to talk to somebody.'

'You knew her real name?'

'Oh, yes. Not at first but she told me a long time ago.'

'And did you know that she owned this house?'

She nodded. 'She wanted to cut my rent but I wouldn't have that. I've never sponged on my friends.' She shifted in her chair to reach a packet of cigarettes from a side table. 'Smoke?'

Wycliffe took his pipe from his pocket and felt for matches. She lit a cigarette and inhaled deeply, trickling the smoke out through nostrils and lips. She must be allowed to tell her story in her own way.

'She had a very unhappy childhood.' The baby-blue eyes were serious and confiding. 'Money isn't everything. It was her father, he was very rich. When she told me first I didn't believe her but afterwards I could tell she was speaking the truth. In any case you could see she was different—'

'Different?'

'Well, educated for one thing.'

'It started with her asking me about my family, what they were like and all that... Her father was a right bastard, he had a taste for under-age girls and once or twice they all got into a hell of a twist to hush it up.

'The boy, her brother, was everything and she was just an afterthought. Her father tried to bring her up very strict and when it didn't work he'd take a stick to her and tell her he was doing it for her own good. I've seen some of that sort. Her mother couldn't do anything with him and she used to console herself with quiet nips from the gin bottle.' She smiled. 'A happy home.'

Wycliffe was puffing away at his pipe, the light from the single electric bulb was yellow and filtered through a plastic shade with a pink fringe.

'I think she felt that she was getting her own back on men, the way she went on. But I used to tell her she was just biting her nose to spite her face—'

'She told you something which you think might have to do with her death?'

She looked at him, her eyes disarmingly frank. 'Well, I don't know, do I?' She tapped ash from her cigarette. 'First going off I persuaded myself it couldn't be anything to do with her being killed but when I thought it over I couldn't be sure and I wouldn't like to think the bastard got away with it because of me.'

'What did she tell you?'

She looked at him with sudden curiosity. 'Are you really a chief super?'

'Yes, why?'

She shrugged. 'I dunno. Anyway, to get back to Chris, she had a boy friend, a regular.'

'She told you?' Wycliffe felt bound to offer encouragement.

She wriggled in her chair to settle her body more comfortably. 'She told me one day when she was feeling a bit down. I said, "A girl like you ought to have a man of your own, get married and have kids." She said, "I've got a man" and I said, "Won't he marry you?" She didn't say anything for a bit then she said, "I think he'd marry me all right but I'm not sure that's what I want."' She looked at Wycliffe in a confiding way, sure that she wouldn't have to explain everything. 'Of course you can imagine what I thought—some old man with one foot in the grave looking for a last kick. But it wasn't like that, this chap was young.'

'She told you about him?'

'Not at first. It was funny really, she was shy about him—her! Then one day she said, "I've never really wanted it before, not until I met him. He's got under my skin, the bastard." A bit later she said, "The funny thing is, he's vicious with it. I never thought I would take that again from any man." She kept coming back to it at different times when she came in. You know what it's like when a girl really falls for a man, she's just got to talk. Once she showed me bruises and I said, "You want to be careful of that sort, my girl." But I mean, she ought to know if anybody did.'

'You've never seen this man?'

'Never.'

'And she never mentioned his name?'

'No, I'd have remembered.'

'Did she tell you about Paul Morris?'

'The Monk?' She laughed. 'That's what she used to call him. She said he was still wet behind the ears. You're not thinking that he—?'

'It's not impossible.'

She looked at him as though he had disappointed her. 'You must be joking!' She reached over and crushed out her cigarette. 'She told me about him and you can take it from me, that boy hardly knows what he's got it for.'

'Did she ever mention going to the Old Custom House with Morris?'

She chuckled, a rich sound of pure enjoyment. 'The bookshop. That was always good for a laugh. Old Jarvis who runs it is a queer and she used to imitate him. She could be a real comic when she felt like it.'

'Apart from that did she tell you anything else about her visits there?'

She stared, frowning, trying to remember. 'No, I don't think so. I know she said she never knew there was so much money in secondhand books.'

Wycliffe produced a photostat of the note he had found in the pocket of Morris's painting coat.

'YOUR GIRL FRIEND IS A WHORE...'

'Did you write that?'

'You don't think that I—'

'No, I don't think so. Have you any idea who might?'

She shook her head.

'Brenda?'

'Brenda wouldn't hurt a fly!'

They sat without speaking for a while. A goods train rattled past at the end of the road, not twenty yards away, and the house vibrated. It seemed to go on

194

interminably. When the sound finally died away the ticking of the alarm clock on the mantelpiece was suddenly intrusive.

'Can you remember anything more about the man?'

Another silence. 'I've been trying to think. He had a car,' she added, abruptly. 'I forget how it came up but she said he had a car.'

Wycliffe was content to sit in the chintz-covered armchair which had a fusty smell, just smoking and waiting.

'She said it several times "He treats me like dirt and I don't know why I stick it." But then she would say, "Of course we're two of a kind". Once she said, "He likes to live dangerously and I suppose I do too".'

'What did she mean by that? How did she live dangerously?'

It was a silly question and she was contemptuous. 'If you know anything about the game you've no need to ask that.'

'She seems to have confided in you more than in anyone else.'

She nodded. 'I'd have rung up before but I didn't want to do the dirt on anybody—not if I was wrong. I mean, after all, he was the only man who ever gave her what she wanted.' She glanced up at the clock. 'I suppose you wouldn't like a cup of something?'

'I must get back. You can't think of anything else?'

'Nothing you don't know already.'

'I suppose he never came to her flat down the road?'

'What do you think?'

'You'll be asked a lot more questions and you may have to make a statement.'

'I'm not coming to the nick.'

'You won't have to, I'll send a WPC.'

'Shall I be in trouble for not having spoken up before?'

'Why should you be? You don't actually *know* anything.'

She came to the door with him and stood on the step, hugging herself against the cold. A woman passing by gave him an odd look as he closed the gate behind him.

He decided to look in on Franks, the pathologist. The pathology laboratories comprised a couple of communicating huts in the grounds of the city's general hospital, a great white wedding-cake of a building with hundreds of square windows. It was visiting time and people were crossing the car park carrying little parcels and bags and bunches of flowers. Wycliffe had difficulty in finding a place for his car but managed to slot it in where a notice said 'Medical Staff Only'.

Franks was in his office dictating notes on the case to his secretary. Franks and his secretaries were notorious—this one was blonde with shoulder length hair and the serene expression of a nun but, by all accounts, she was following the same path as her predecessors. What it was that appealed to these young women about the roly-poly doctor had escaped Wycliffe's notice. Unless it was the romance of the macabre.

Franks went on dictating, waving Wycliffe to a chair. He was full of more or less harmless affectations and his white office was one of them, even the desk, the chairs and the filing cabinets were white. His rows of books, which happened to include many with red or blue bindings, provided a startling splash of colour. The astringent odour of formalin penetrated through from the laboratory adding to the unreal atmosphere of the place. Why did it suggest to Wycliffe the absurd notion of an administrative office in Heaven?

Franks finished his dictation, dismissed his secretary and turned to Wycliffe almost in the same breath. 'Subject male, probably between twenty-five and thirty years old. Height about one hundred and eighty-five centimetres—you see, we've gone metric —but it means that he was tall.

'As to the cause of death, he was shot.' He took a small specimen tube from his desk drawer and placed it on the top. In the tube a bullet rested on a pad of cotton wool. 'Don't ask me, I've never seen one like it before.'

'Shot!' Wycliffe had been taken by surprise.

'As I removed the bullet from his skull that seems a reasonable deduction. The bullet penetrated the palatine process of the right superior maxillary bone, ricocheted in the skull vault and ended by splintering but not penetrating the left parietal near the coronal suture.'

'In other words he was shot through the roof of the mouth, that usually means suicide in my book.'

'Perhaps you read the wrong book. The fact that the bullet failed to penetrate the roof of the skull made me look further and I found definite signs that it had grazed the inside of the mandible on the right side which would be consistent with the gun having been held under the chin, an uncommon method for suicide, you'll agree.'

'Or for murder.'

Franks nodded. 'As you say.'

'So?'

Franks rearranged his crystal pen tray and his white pig-skin blotter. 'I wouldn't care to have to back this in court but I *think* the bullet was fired from lower down, about the level of the chap's navel. The ribs are in a very bad state but I'm of the opinion that the bullet scored two or three of them.'

Wycliffe was impressed. He lit his pipe and waited until it was drawing before speaking. 'A struggle, in the course of which a shot was fired.'

'A fatal shot,' Franks added. 'I would go along with that. If the bullet was fired low down and followed a path which penetrated clothing and scored several ribs before entering under the chin it might account for the fact that the residual momentum was insufficient for a final penetration of the skull table.'

'The question now is, whose gun?'

Franks smiled smugly. 'Outside my province. Have you any idea who the chap is?'

'Your description fits with a young chap called Morris, an architect, who's been missing since the evening of the fire. We shall have to try to get some sort of identification so anything from you will be welcome—dentition, old fractures, skeletal abnormalities—anything.'

Franks shook his head. 'Nothing, except that he seems to have had a perfect set of teeth which is rare these days. I say, seems, because there is one odd feature, the top four incisors and the left canine are missing–'

'That hardly sounds like a perfect set of teeth.'

'No, but to the best of my belief, he lost those five teeth with considerable damage to the maxillary bones at about the time he died, perhaps a little before, perhaps after.'

'Not due to the bullet?'

'No, the path of the bullet is clearly defined and did not traverse the actual tooth row at any point.'

'Damage caused by the fall when the floors collapsed?'

Franks shrugged. 'It's possible, but it seems odd; the lower jaw, for example, is undamaged save by the fire.'

'A blow before death, perhaps in the struggle?'

Franks looked pompous. 'I would favour that possibility though I would not be prepared to testify to it in court. The blow would have needed to be particularly vicious. Obviously there would have been no point in administering such a blow after death.'

'So you think it was a blow?'

'Entirely between ourselves, I do.'

Wycliffe was thoughtful. 'Nothing else you can tell me?'

Franks was fiddling with the tube containing the bullet, rolling it between his finger and thumb. He loved to dramatize his rôle. 'There could be. I have not yet completed the autopsy. I was able to retrieve small amounts of undamaged tissue and I may be able to give you a grouping—not necessarily based on the blood, but equally valid.'

Wycliffe stood up. 'Good. I'll leave you to it.'

When he left the hospital visitors were leaving too and he was caught up in a long line of slow-moving traffic. A Salvation Army band playing carols near the hospital gate reminded him again that tomorrow would be Christmas Eve. One more year when he had given Helen no help with the preparations. When he got home tonight the twins would be there, they had been staying with friends since the end of the university term. He felt depressed, deprived was a better word, a little resentful that his job seemed to cut him off. It wasn't only the long hours, he was emotionally cut off. For days or even weeks together when he was on a big case he seemed to be living other people's lives, to be immersed in their problems, prying into their secrets. Helen had said that a doctor must feel the same, but a doctor is involved in many cases at the same time and detachment is easier.

The traffic sorted itself out at the roundabout where six roads met.

Two killings and arson for good measure.

Somebody had to warn Mrs Morris that it was probably her son's body which lay on Dr Franks's dissecting table. He pulled into a parking space to consult a map of the city. Spencer Gardens where the Morrises lived was regarded as a respectable neighbourhood, the people who lived there got monthly pay cheques instead of weekly pay packets and their kids did not commonly smash up telephone boxes or nick cigarettes. The houses were semi-detached and between each pair there were two garages set back from the road. People who lived in Spencer Gardens read the *Daily Mail* or even the *Telegraph*. Most of the sitting-room windows had the curtains drawn back and displayed Christmas trees elaborately decorated and lit.

Wycliffe drove slowly along the street trying to make out the numbers. Number forty-two, when he came to it, seemed tatty compared with the rest. By the light of the street lamp he could see that the brickwork had not been pointed and that paint was flaking off the gate and the front door. He had to ring three times before a light went on in the hall, he heard movement then the door was opened by a tall, gaunt woman wearing a woollen two-piece which hung on her as if on a hanger.

He showed his warrant card. 'Detective Chief Superintendent Wycliffe.'

She made no response and continued to block the doorway.

'May I come in?'

She stood aside and switched on the light in a room to the left of the front door. It was a sitting-room and it looked as though it had been neither used nor cleaned in years. A copper pot containing dried grasses and the dusty, faded feathers of some exotic bird stood in the centre of a large round table made of a yellow wood. A low-powered bulb covered by a pink satin shade hung low over the table so that the rest of the room was barely visible. She did not invite him to sit down.

'I've come about your son, Paul Morris.'

'He's not here.'

'I know.'

'His home is not good enough for him, he just uses it like an hotel.' They were stock phrases that she used whenever the occasion arose.

'Perhaps we could sit down?'

'If you like.' But she remained standing as though waiting for him to go.

'It is quite possible that your son has been involved in a serious accident.'

She seemed not to have heard him, she was arranging the ornamental grasses.

'It's a question of identification...I'm very much afraid that it may be your son.'

'An accident, you say?'

'It's possible that your son has been killed.'

'No.' She spoke without emphasis but with certainty while she smoothed the table runner with the edge of her palm to remove creases.

'You don't know where your son is?'

'I never know where he is. If you ask me, he's just gone off like his father. Like father like son, that's what I always say. He'll come back if it suits him.' She gave a dry, sarcastic little laugh. 'His father went when Paul was fourteen. You didn't know that, did you?'

'I know that you are a widow, Mrs Morris.'

'Nothing of the kind. I'm no widow, not as far as I know. His father just walked out—vanished. One morning after breakfast—through that door. He went out and never came back.' She massaged her threadbare sleeves with bony hands. The room was bitterly cold.

'I didn't let it interfere with Paul's chances, he's an architect—qualified.' She threw out the statement like a challenge. 'I gave him every chance in spite of his father. It was a struggle and you'd think he'd be grateful, but I never see him, off every morning after he's bolted down his breakfast, evenings, week-ends.'

Wycliffe felt that he must keep running to stay where he was. 'In case it is your son I'd like to ask you one or two questions.'

She smiled in a way that made him feel uncomfortable. 'It isn't him, I tell you.' At last she sat down, on the edge of one of the upright chairs. 'His father was an accountant, he worked with a firm called Martin, Spender and Jukes. After he'd gone I found he'd given them a month's notice. He wouldn't let the firm down.'

'Did your son ever break a limb?'

The question focused her attention for a moment. 'Paul? No, never.'

'Did he ever have any sort of operation?'

'No, nothing like that. He was a perfect child; perfect, physically, the doctor said when he was born. Perfect.'

'Had he lost any teeth? Did he ever go to the dentist?'

'Paul has never been to the dentist in his life. No need, he has perfect teeth. He has a little gap between two of his front teeth and I used to tell him when he was little that it meant he would die rich.'

Wycliffe was beaten. 'Could I see his room?'

'If you want to.' Her composure was unnerving. 'It's on the left at the top of the stairs.'

The carpet on the stairs was threadbare and the wallpaper had faded to an indeterminate shade. The room was a back room, it was bare, a single bed, a tiny wardrobe and a chest of drawers. A cheap bookcase contained mainly works on architecture but there were several physical culture books including three or four on judo. Chest expanders hung on a hook behind the door and there was a species of rowing machine on the floor. These things surprised Wycliffe who had thought of Morris as a weedy youth.

She had followed him upstairs and she now stood in the doorway, watching, as though some invisible barrier stopped her from crossing the threshold.

'Is your son keen on sport?'

'Not on sport. Only on judo, it was the one thing apart from his work which interested him at school.'

Wycliffe lacked the courage to make any sort of search but it would have to be done some time. 'Where does he do his painting?'

She looked at him as though he had taken leave of his senses. 'Painting? He's never done any painting since he was at the junior school.'

'You say that he is not at home much, does he sleep away from home?'

'Never.'

'What about holidays?'

'Just the same—off all day, I never see him except when he's getting up or going to bed.'

'Does he never ask you to go out with him?'

She made a curious sound, half between a laugh and a sneer. 'He used to, but where would I want to go?'

She saw him to the door and stood on the doorstep until he had closed the gate. 'Thank you, Mrs Morris. I will keep in touch.'

She did not bother to reply.

The air was sharp with frost, clear and still. The sky overhead was almost saxe blue. In a house opposite a family was watching television with the curtains undrawn and the room lit only by the light of the flickering screen and the coloured lamps on the Christmas tree.

Wycliffe decided to go home. The city seemed empty, the Christmas lights shone over empty streets. The only sign of revelry came from the pubs in snatches of song as he passed. He stopped at a newsvendor's pitch, the man had gone home but he had left a few papers and a box for money. He bought a paper and glanced at the headlines in the light of a street lamp. BODY IN BLAZE—LINK WITH STANLEY STREET MURDER? After an account of the fire and the finding of the body the report went on:

'The police are investigating the possibility of a link between this tragedy and the murder of Christine Powell on Wednesday evening. The body found in the débris of the fire had not been identified at the time of going to press but there is informed speculation that it may turn out to be that of a young professional man employed by a local firm.'

As he neared home a half-moon rode high in the sky above the estuary and the Watch House stood out white in the landscape. The old banger which belonged to the twins was parked across the entrance to the garage so that he had to leave his car on the gravel. But his wife and his daughter kissed him under the mistletoe and his son handed him a glass of sherry.

CHAPTER EIGHT

Lesley Birch, the prostitute, quoting the dead girl, had said, 'The funny thing is he's vicious with it. I never thought I would take that again from any man...'

And Andrew Jarvis had told him, 'Derek isn't above taking advantage of a situation like that; in fact, I sometimes think he has a cruel streak in his nature.'

The words sounded inside his head as though they were being spoken, he could recall the tone and the manner of their delivery so exactly. Yet it was only now that he linked the two statements together.

It was half past five on Christmas Eve morning and he had been lying awake for more than an hour. In the stillness he had heard a clock, somewhere across the water, strike four then, after an infinity of time, five. The night-light by the telephone at his bedside played tricks on his eyes. Sometimes its pale radiance seemed to fill the whole room then it would shrink to a point of light so intense that it hurt his eyes and confused his sense of direction.

Derek Robson.

But why should he kill the girl? Killing is, presumably, the logical end of the sadist's progress but the crime had not been notably sadistic. And why would Robson set fire to the flat in Middle Street?

Paul Morris. The Monk.

Morris is missing and there is a dead man of his approximate age and height in the mortuary.

Robson is missing too. Missing? Well, nobody seems to know where he is but his car is still at the Old Custom House. Morris and Robson are both 'between twenty-five and thirty' and both are tall.

Coincidence. Imagination has been the downfall of more than one good jack.

A struggle and a shot, a fatal shot. Was the fire a vain attempt to cover the killing? Or was the incendiary disturbed in his work?

If he lay very still and listened intently he could just hear the clang of a bell-buoy out to sea, and, with the eye of his mind, he could watch the slow undulant surge of black water, gleaming in the darkness.

There was a gap, he must have dozed.

'I never knew there was so much money in secondhand books.' So much money—

'We sell books of antiquarian interest and importance... We specialize in foreign books, mainly French. Three or four times a year Derek takes the van across the ferry... Our last consignment, we haven't had a chance to sort them yet.'

He wished that he had taken a closer look at those books. But why?

Helen whispered tensely in her sleep and he put his hand on her thigh.

Christine Powell had been uniquely eligible as a victim. She qualified as a tart, as a blackmailer paying off substantial business interests, as a woman who seemed to delight in putting men through the hoop. Added to that she had taken up with a man who seemed to have specialized sexual needs.

For the twentieth time he decided to clear his mind, to 'go blank' and so fall asleep.

Any one of the dubious crowd she mixed with might have killed her and any one of them might have decided to protect himself by setting alight to the Middle Street flat. Why should Morris go there? Or Robson?

Powell... Salt... Bates... His thoughts were wandering, he was getting further away, losing the thread instead of following it.

'He has perfect teeth...'

'The top four incisors and the left canine are missing...considerable damage to the maxillary bones at or about the time he died, perhaps a little before, perhaps after.'

'So you think it was a blow?'

'Obviously there would have been no point in administering such a blow after death.'

Powell... Salt... Bates... Harkness... Purvis... Powell... The names were sounding in his head in time with the swinging bell. Once more he could see the black water rising and falling, rising and falling. This time he slept.

The alarm clock blared insanely and Helen switched it off. Then she switched on the bedside lamp and, as always, turned to kiss him on the forehead. As always, her lips were cool.

'Slept well, dear?'

'Bloody! And you?'

'Like a log.'

Their new surroundings certainly agreed with Helen. He got up, pulled on his dressing-gown and went over to the window. Standing with the curtains behind him he could feel the cold coming off the glass. The stars were still out, not a cloud anywhere. Fine and frosty. He went back and switched on the radio.

'The Bank of England says that it will be a record spending Christmas with an increase in the note circulation of eight per cent... The weather is set fair, not, perhaps a traditional Christmas for, say the Met Office, snow is unlikely anywhere in the British Isles; but it will be cold and the old Yule log will come in handy if you can find one and you have somewhere to burn it. Now for the News Headlines at seven-thirty precisely...

'A Union spokesman for the car strikers said last night that officials will be available all over Christmas, ready to enter into meaningful discussions with the management...

'In the Powell murder case police say that the man whose charred remains were found after a fire in the murdered girl's flat had been shot at close range—'

'Shall I go first?' The same question on

every working morning of his married life. As though Helen would take possession of the bathroom before him. Fortunately now, they had two, one on the ground floor.

He remembered that he had thought a good deal about the case during the night. As he bathed and shaved he tried to recall those thoughts without much success. He had the disturbing feeling amounting almost to conviction that he had made a discovery or reached a conclusion but he could not focus his recollection.

By the time he set out on his drive to the city the sun was above the horizon and the sky was turquoise blue. People were going to work with a cheerful air. A queue of lorries lined the street to the pannier market. WPC Saxton was waiting for him with his post and the chrysanthemums had been rearranged. Instead of attending to the post he went to the duty room. DC Dixon was there.

'I've found him, sir.' The satisfaction in his voice was unmistakable.

'Who?'

'The lame man who was with the prostitute in the top flat on the night of the murder.'

It had been a question of tying up a

loose end, or so they had thought.

'I brought him in this morning, sir, he's in number four interview room. I think you might like to hear what he's got to say.'

Dixon's little lame man was sitting at a bare deal table, dejected and resigned. He had on the mackintosh he had been wearing when Brenda picked him up.

'Mr Watkins, sir. Mr Watkins is an unemployed bricklayer.'

'Mr Watkins?'

'That's me, sir.'

'I think you have something to tell me.'

He was probably no older than Wycliffe but his face was lined and seemed to have been cast in a mould of permanent sadness. He looked at Dixon, standing near the door, 'I told the lad, sir.'

Wycliffe saw the flush on Dixon's cheeks. 'Now tell me.'

The man lifted his shoulders in a gesture of helplessness. 'It's just that I met him, when I was going in to that house he was coming out.'

'You were going into 9 Stanley Street, is that right?'

'It was the first time. I swear to God! And it will be the last.' He wiped his lips with a grubby handkerchief. 'As I was going to open the door, he opened it first—'

'Who are you talking about, Mr Watkins?'

'The young man.'

'What young man?'

Watkins' brow furrowed with the effort required of him. 'Well, he was in a grey overcoat, a tall young fellow, thin—'

'You recognized him?'

'Not then, sir, but now I know who he was. Mr...this young man showed me a photograph and then I knew him.'

'Mr Dixon showed you a photograph of a young man and you recognized him as being the same man you had seen leaving the flat?'

'I think so, sir, and I saw then that it was this architect chap. I mean, I remembered that I'd seen him before on building sites when I was a brickie.'

'Mr Dixon has your address?'

'Oh yes, sir.'

'Then we can ask you to come in and make a statement later. Thank you, Mr Watkins.'

The lame man, not quite sure what had happened to him, got up and after looking at the two policemen doubtfully, made off down the passage. The expression on Dixon's face made Wycliffe want to laugh. 'It's not the end of the world, Dixon.'

Dixon shook his head. 'I don't get it, sir.'

'Think what would happen if we let Watkins go into court. He says he saw a young man in a grey overcoat leaving the house in Stanley Street. He told me a moment ago that he didn't recognize him at the time but when you showed him a photograph of Morris he recognized it as the architect chap he had seen on building sites and he *thought* it was the same man he had seen coming out of the house. The Defence would accuse us of having led the witness and they would make mincemeat out of poor old Watkins in the box.'

'So we need an identity parade, sir.'

'If we find Morris it would be an idea but even if Watkins picked him out of a parade it could be argued that he was identifying the man he saw in your photograph rather than the one he saw in Stanley Street.'

Dixon looked crestfallen. 'I've balled up a good witness.'

Wycliffe grinned. 'I wouldn't have called

Watkins a good witness but next time don't be in such a hurry to show a witness photographs.'

'I'm very sorry, sir.'

'I expect you are but don't dwell on it, I've got more important things for you to think about. You'd better come with me.' They walked along the corridor to the lift together.

'By the way, how did you pick him up?'

'Tim Parnell, landlord of The Joiners in Prince's Street recognized his description. It seems he's a harmless old boy, his wife left him a few years back and he's lived on his own ever since. Last year he had an accident and injured his leg, since then he hasn't been able to climb ladders.'

Back in his office Wycliffe picked up the telephone and asked to be put through to Mr Winter of Lloyd and Winter. Mr Winter was distressed.

'Disappeared? But where could he have gone and why?... Yes, a first class young man, a very promising architect... Yes, we have tried to keep him by the offer of a junior partnership... Well worth it... Yes, he seems to have a thing about his mother, almost a morbid sense of responsibility...

Between you and me I think the old girl imposes on the lad... No, I know nothing about his private life, he is not at all communicative, quite the reverse... If he wasn't such a good architect it would have held him back—none of the social graces... As you and I know only too well a good many professional men owe their success to the nineteenth hole... No trouble, a pleasure... And to you.'

Wycliffe dropped the receiver with a grimace. He had never had nor wished to have any part in the freemasonry of successful professional men. If he had done he would probably have made chief constable but he had no regrets about that either.

'Do you play golf, Dixon?'

'Golf? No, sir.'

'Perhaps you should take it up.'

'I'll bear it in mind, sir.' The boy was learning fast.

'I want you to go to Morris's home. Be nice to his mother and listen to what she tells you. If you go the right way about it you won't have any difficulty in searching through his stuff without upsetting her. Report directly to me.'

Dixon flushed with pleasure.

When Dixon had gone Wycliffe went down to the yard behind the headquarters buildings where there were garages, stores and a workshop. All the material brought back from the fire was stored in two garages. Larger items had been placed on the floor against the walls while smaller things were laid out on trestle tables with some attempt at classification. Sergeant Scales was there with a constable and a young man from Forensic, an expert on fires.

Wycliffe prowled about looking at the exhibits with a glazed expression. He paused before half-a-dozen metal drawers, scorched and distorted by the fire, which had clearly come from a filing cabinet.

'These drawers, why did you take them out of the cabinet?'

'We didn't sir, they were all over the place, all we did was to collect them together.'

The man from Forensic, who had not previously worked with Wycliffe, volunteered, 'The chap who started the fire must have emptied out the contents of the drawers to make sure that everything in them got burnt. You can see that the paint has been burnt from the parts of the drawers which would normally have been protected by the cabinet.'

All he got for his pains was a cold hard stare which made him feel uncomfortable.

On the tables there were heaps of pottery scraps, twisted and discoloured cutlery, bits of electrical wizardry which must have come from a record player or a television set or both. There were all manner of tortured bits of metal which had once been parts of chairs and other furniture and the workings of a clock. All the débris had been sifted and the 'finds' brought to these sheds. It was like an archaeological dig.

'No sign of a gun?'

Scales came over. 'Not yet, sir, and they're almost through on the site. We did find this though.' He pointed to a specimen tube containing a bullet which could have been the twin of the one Wycliffe had seen in Dr Franks' laboratory.

'So there must have been two shots.'

'Looks like it, sir. I'm sending this over to Waddington for comparison and report.' The area force had no ballistics expert on the staff but they made use of a local gunsmith who had a national reputation and had testified in several cases for the Crown.

In the middle of one of the tables, apparently perfect, scarcely tarnished, were two bronze elephants, exquisitely modelled and standing eighteen inches or more at the shoulders.

'Nice elephants.'

'Sir?' It was the man from Forensic.

'I said, these are nice elephants.'

'Very nice, sir.'

It was from such exchanges that the Wycliffe legend grew and some said that the *non sequitur* was a deliberate and cultivated eccentricity. In fact, it usually followed, as now, an occasion when he had snubbed somebody and wanted to say something mildly placatory but could think of nothing.

He tried again. 'When can I expect your report on the fire?'

'I think it's on the way to you, sir, but I can give you the gist of it.' The young man took a deep breath as though about to recite. 'From our study of the incendiary device recovered—'

'You mean the candle and the bucket?'

'Yes, sir. Well, as I was saying, from our study we came to the conclusion that it would have taken about five-and-a-half hours for the device to become effective—'

'For the candle to burn down to the paraffin?'

'That is correct, sir. The fire, as I understand it, was discovered at 0340 hours, not long after it had started, so, if the other devices were similar they must have been activated around 2200 hours.'

In other words the fire-raiser had lit his candles and cleared off before Wycliffe arrived but the one in the bedroom had blown out. When Wycliffe was peering in through the glass door of the kitchen the dead man was already lying in the front room and Forensic's 'incendiary devices' had already been 'activated'.

'How much paraffin was there in the bucket?'

'About one point five litres, sir.'

'In translation?'

'About a third of a gallon.'

'So a gallon of paraffin could have done the lot?'

'That is so, sir.'

Wycliffe continued to browse around like a bargain hunter in a jumble sale. There seemed to be a lot of fragments of porcelain figurines and Scales, who knew about such things, confirmed that the girl must have been a collector. 'I think this will interest you, sir. I've just come across it in the lot which has just arrived.'

It was a steel identity disc on a chain, one of the links of the chain had been broken near the clasp. On one side of the disc an inscription read: Derek Robson 4.XI.44

Robson! If the disc had come from the body—

'I suppose the chain could have snapped as the body fell,' Scales suggested, uninhibited by preconceived notions.

Wycliffe changed the subject. 'I suppose a lot of this stuff comes from the tobacconist's?'

'We've done our best and he's been quite helpful considering everything but we can't be sure.'

'It doesn't matter.'

'There are sacks of carbonized paper and card, it would take months to go through it all.'

'Don't waste time over it. Forget it.' Wycliffe seemed to have lost interest. He walked over to the scorched and twisted remains of an oil heater. 'Was this the tobacconist's?'

'He says not, it must have belonged to the flat. She had night-storage heaters and electric fires but she probably kept this in case of a power failure.'

Wycliffe walked slowly back to his office. He used the stairs and not the lift and he seemed unaware of the people who passed him. Sergeant Bourne, the young man who seemed destined to be chief constable, was waiting for him in WPC Saxton's office. Wycliffe thought, not entirely without malice, what a splendid pair they would make.

'I've made some progress, sir, and I thought you might wish to hear.'

With a gesture Wycliffe swept him into his office. Bourne had been busy. The city librarian had put him on to a real bibliophile, an elderly gentleman who lived in a large house about thirty miles up the coast. Bourne had been to see him the previous evening.

'He knew Jarvis?'

'Very well, sir. Jarvis is, apparently, quite a figure in the book world.'

'As a dealer?'

Bourne frowned. 'He is certainly known as a dealer but Mr Baldwin—that's the gentleman's name—knew him best as a collector of illustrated books and prints. Apparently he has been collecting for years and he had contributed numerous papers to the journals. Until recently, the last two or three years, he built up his collection from items he happened to come across in the course of business, usually for much less than their market value; now he attends major sales and he has purchased three or four items at considerable cost.'

'How considerable?'

'Mr Baldwin estimates that his purchases in the past three years must have cost him many thousands of pounds.'

'I never knew there was so much money in secondhand books.'

'I beg your pardon, sir?'

'Never mind.' He congratulated Bourne and told him to return to his normal duties.

Whatever else the finding of Robson's identity disc might mean it left little doubt that he had visited the Middle Street flat. Could it, after all, be his body in the mortuary? If so, what had happened to Morris?

He picked up the telephone and put through a call to Andrew Jarvis. 'I wondered if you have had any news of your assistant?'

There was a brief silence then Jarvis

228

spoke, tense and anxious. 'No, I have not. As a matter of fact I was about to ring you. I'm afraid that I was not entirely frank when you were here yesterday...' He waited for some comment from Wycliffe and when none was forthcoming, went on, 'I wonder if I might come over to explain?'

'There is no need, Mr Jarvis, I shall be coming to see you during the day... Sometime today, I can't say exactly when. As it is Christmas Eve I suppose you are likely to be there all day?'

Jarvis agreed.

'There is one question, does Robson wear dentures?'

'Dentures?' Jarvis sounded surprised by the question, as well he might. 'Yes, he has a small plate, four of his top front teeth were knocked out when he was a lad. He is quite sensitive about it.'

'What about his other teeth?'

'As far as I know he has excellent teeth but I really can't see—'

Wycliffe rang off. The 'dear boy' interpolations were notably absent. Jarvis was a worried man. So much the better. He was on the point of putting out a general call but changed his mind. Instead

229

he arranged for the Old Custom House to be watched.

He worked at his reorganization plan for a while but his thoughts were elsewhere. From time to time he walked to the window and stood watching the seemingly endless flow of traffic into the city. Twice WPC Saxton came in with queries about sections of the report she was typing and she had the surprising impression that he was glad to be interrupted. Her third intrusion was to tell him that DC Dixon was waiting to report.

But Dixon had little to tell. He had met with no difficulty in dealing with Mrs Morris. 'She couldn't have cared less what I did. Have you ever seen her, sir? It was incredible. If I'd been missing for twenty-four hours my mother would have been calling out the marines.' All he had found of possible interest were three photographs in a yellow, paper wallet. 'I thought I ought to bring them though they probably don't mean anything.'

Wycliffe spread them on his desk, three colour snaps. The first had been taken on a beach and showed Robson, in swimming trunks, with his arms round two girls in bikinis. One of the girls, petite and smiling, was Christine Powell; the other, sturdy and grinning dutifully into the camera, seemed familiar but Wycliffe could not immediately place her. Then he remembered, it was almost certainly the freckled Irish girl from the café in Bear Street where Jarvis and Robson got their meals. The second snap was a clever or lucky one of Christine Powell standing under the cedar in dappled sunlight. She was looking up into the branches, apparently unaware of the camera.

'I found them in one of the drawers in his chest-of-drawers. I showed them to his mother and she said she had never seen the girls or the man in her life. "How would you expect me to know who he spends his time with?"' Dixon could not resist imitating her tone and manner.

Wycliffe was looking at the third snap. Again the girl from the café, this time sitting in the driving seat of a red Mini. She had her head through the open window, laughing. She appealed to Wycliffe, there was something practical, even earthy about her, the sort of girl who might have done Morris a lot of good, giving him the kicks and the ha'pence he so badly needed.

Just as he was leaving for lunch a telex

came through from Criminal Records. Nothing known of Andrew Jarvis but Robson had a record. Two convictions for violence against women. He had served two years and he had not troubled to change his name.

Wycliffe went to lunch with Gill at Teague's and they had to wait for a table. The set meal was roast turkey and Christmas pudding, there was a sprig of holly on each table and paper chains were suspended from the ceiling. Already Wycliffe resented the invasion of the place by 'casuals'.

Gill had been spending time on the dead girl's clients and associates, in particular, Harkness, Purvis, Salt and Bates. He was morose. 'Reluctantly, I think we've got to count Salt out of this one, he had a lot to gain from continued association with the girl. Purvis and Harkness were being blackmailed, in a mild sort of way, for inside information, not for money.' Gill sipped his beer in a preoccupied way, 'It was all fairly low-key, no high drama as far as I can see and no reason for it.'

'What did she have on them?'

'She threatened Harkness that she would send naughty pictures to his wife, the pictures probably didn't exist but the threat was enough. With Purvis she said she had evidence, and he believed her, of a bit of dirty work he was involved in six or seven years back.' Gill became the burly rock-faced contractor. '"Of course I've never taken advantage of my position on the council to further my own interest but a few years back I allowed myself to oppose a development (a foolish one) which would have been inconvenient to a friend of mine."

'"And your friend rewarded you. How much?"

'Purvis wasn't anxious to talk figures but in the end he did. "Five thousand. It was several years ago and we were going through a sticky patch at the time, the money came in handy." The bastard was less ashamed of the fact than of the amount. He thought his integrity rated a higher bid.'

'How did you get all this?'

Gill gave one of his horrific grins. 'I put the fear of God into the bastard and I enjoyed every minute of it.' He emptied his glass and signalled the waitress for another. He rarely had to ask for anything twice where a woman was concerned and the

233

beer came with gratifying promptitude.

'So none of them killed the girl?'

'In my opinion, no.'

'To tidy the thing up we need alibis for Middle Street. We can't be certain that it was the same operator.'

Gill nodded. 'I've attended to that and as far as I can see they are all in the clear. Bates and his girl friend were at the *Nite Spot* in Fuller Road. At least that's what they say and so does Alec Bose, the owner. Purvis was at a council meeting and Harkness was attending a bun-fight organized by the chartered surveyors. Salt's alibi is thinner, he was at home with his wife but, for once, I believe him.' He took a deep draught of his beer. 'No report on the gun?'

'Nothing useful. Sure to be unregistered. Waddington says that, judging from the condition of the first bullet—he hadn't seen the second when he made his report—it was almost certainly from an old service revolver from the First World War. He thinks it was a Belgian gun, it's an odd calibre. He also said that the gun couldn't have been cleaned or fired in years.'

'That's what I like about experts,' Gill said. 'Helpful.'

CHAPTER NINE

Before going to see Jarvis Wycliffe called on the girl in the Bear Street café. Her last lunchtime customer was paying his bill. 'Thank *you*, sir. Shall we see you tomorrow?' The open smile and easy manner must be good for trade. She followed her customer to the door and shot the bolts behind him then she turned to Wycliffe. 'Well?'

Wycliffe laid his three snapshots on one of the café tables and she looked at them cursorily. 'Where did you get those?'

Wycliffe pointed to the one of Robson with the two girls. 'You didn't tell me that you were on such good terms.'

'You didn't ask me.'

'Are you fond of him?'

'I suppose you could say that.'

'I understand that he has gone away for Christmas.'

'Really?'

'Didn't you know?'

'I haven't seen him around.'

235

He realized that he would get more by frontal attack than by subterfuge. 'How well do you know Robson?'

'I know him.'

'Do you sleep with him?'

'Sometimes.'

'I suppose Morris took this snap?'

She nodded. 'As far as I can remember.'

'Did the four of you go round much together?'

'Not a lot. Now and then Derek would take us all somewhere in his car, usually on a Sunday afternoon.'

'Two couples, you and Robson, Christine and Morris.'

She was clearing the tables as they talked, stacking dishes on a tray. 'You know it wasn't like that.'

'How was it?'

'Christine didn't give a damn for Paul Morris, she collected men like kids collect stamps and Paul was an odd specimen she happened to pick up.'

'And Robson?'

'That was different. No woman will ever collect Derek.'

'So you and Christine Powell were after the same man?'

She turned to him, her snub nose

wrinkled with distaste. 'If you want to put it that way, but if you're trying to say that I was jealous then you're wrong. I knew Derek wasn't the sort to settle for one woman, if it hadn't been Christine Powell it would have been somebody else.' She lifted the heavy tray on to the counter. 'I'm not daft, I knew there was no future in it for me.'

Wycliffe pointed to the snap of her sitting in the driving seat of a red Mini. 'Your car?'

'Mine, my dad's, I drive it anyway.' She was standing beside him, waiting for him to go. 'If you've got no more questions...'

Wycliffe felt sure she was under stress, her anxiety to be rid of him arose from more than a desire to get on with her work. She had not asked him any questions. Surely, in the circumstances, this was unnatural?

'You've read about the fire in Middle Street?'

'I heard about it on the News.'

'You know that we found a body?'

'Yes.'

'In the débris we also found an identity disc with Derek Robson's name on it.'

'I see.' Her face and voice were both expressionless.

'When did you last see Robson?'

She hesitated as though trying to recall. 'It must have been Thursday evening when I took in their meal.' He said nothing and she went on, 'You can't tell for sure who it is?'

'Not yet, no.' He was reluctant to leave, sensing that there was something which she was holding back but unable to guess what it might be. 'If you decide that you have something to tell me you can telephone police headquarters at any time.'

She looked blank. 'I don't know what you mean.'

When Wycliffe arrived at the bookshop Jarvis had a customer who was trying to decide whether or not to spend his money on a set of Fabre's *Souvenirs Entomologiques*. Jarvis had clearly lost interest in the transaction before Wycliffe arrived, now he almost drove the poor man out of his shop. He shut the door behind him and reversed the card from OPEN to CLOSED.

'I'm glad you've come. Please come into my office.' He was agitated and his movements were quick and jerky. 'I'm very worried.'

'About your assistant?'

'About Derek, yes. I ought to have been more frank with you but I didn't want to stir up a lot of fuss about nothing.'

In his little office he lifted a pile of books off the seat of a cane-bottomed chair for Wycliffe and sat, himself, in the swivel chair by his desk. 'As I told you, Derek goes off for a day or two now and then but he always tells me well in advance to make sure that it will be convenient and he always lets me know when to expect him back.'

'Not this time?'

'No. I had no idea that he was going and I don't know when to expect him back.' He clasped his hands together, studied his paired thumbs then unclasped them again. 'I'd better tell you.' He turned in his chair to face Wycliffe with an expression of great candour. 'The night before last—Thursday night—we had a difference of opinion about the business—you might call it a row, I suppose—and after our evening meal Derek went out without a word. That was the last I saw of him.' Jarvis paused then added. 'But I heard him.

I'd gone to bed and I heard him come in around midnight. I sleep in a room on this floor, along the passage. To be honest, I thought he was drunk, he made such a noise. He seemed to blunder about in the little hall for a time then, finally, I heard him going up the stairs.'

'And then?'

'I must have fallen asleep.' He looked apologetic. 'I suppose I must have woken from time to time during the night but I certainly heard nothing more of Derek. It was not until after ten o'clock next morning when he had failed to put in an appearance that I went up to his room and found that his bed had not been slept in.'

'He has never done such a thing before?'

'Never!'

Wycliffe felt sure that Jarvis had still not told him all there was to tell. 'Yesterday you went to some trouble to conceal all this, Mr Jarvis, today you seem anxious to tell me—why the change?'

Jarvis swung round to face his desk. 'Well dear boy, twenty-four hours have gone by with no news.'

'The truth, Mr Jarvis.'

Jarvis looked intensely miserable. 'You

are right, of course, dear boy, but I don't want to make trouble for Derek.'

'By being reticent in a murder case you are making trouble for yourself.'

'He took some books of mine with him and that convinces me that he has no intention of coming back.'

'Valuable books?'

'That is beside the point, I am not primarily concerned about the books.'

'All the same, were the books valuable?'

Jarvis still could not bring himself to give a straight answer. 'You can't price old books like groceries, dear boy.'

'How much were the books worth?' Wycliffe was becoming aggressive, impatient with Jarvis's evasions and pretensions which made it difficult to decide whether his story as a whole should be believed.

The bookseller sighed. 'We are talking of many hundreds.'

'Negotiable?'

Jarvis pursed his thin lips. 'In the right market; the books were obviously chosen with this in mind. None of them was sufficiently rare to draw attention and might have been bought over the counter by any good dealer.'

Wycliffe was watching him closely, half convinced that the tale was just another fabrication. 'I shall want a list of the missing books.'

'But I'm making no complaint—'

Wycliffe snapped: 'That's up to you. If you tell me that Robson has gone off with these books they may help us to trace him and that is my concern.'

The little office had only a tiny, rather murky, window high up over the desk. It was like being at the bottom of a well and Wycliffe got up to switch on the light without asking leave. The action was not lost on Jarvis.

'Robson didn't take his car with him which must be worth more than the books, how do you explain that?'

'I can't explain it, dear boy, it is very puzzling.'

'When Robson came in at midnight you heard him but you didn't see him, is that right?'

'Quite right, I told you I was in bed—'

'So that it might not have been him?'

Jarvis stiffened as though struck by an entirely new possibility. 'But who else could it have been? I mean, whoever it was had a key.'

'An identity disc with Robson's name on it was found in the débris of the Middle Street fire.'

'Good God! Does that mean—'

'I don't know what it means but there is a possibility that it is Robson's body which lies in the mortuary.'

Jarvis shook his head hopelessly. 'I don't know what to think.' He stared at his desk in silence for a while before turning again to Wycliffe. 'But if it wasn't Derek I heard, who could it have been?'

'Paul Morris?'

'Paul? But why should Paul—?'

'If he had shot Robson and wanted to get away.'

Jarvis stared at him without speaking for a while then, with apparent reluctance, he said, 'What you are saying begins to make a horrible kind of sense.

'The books, the car—Paul knew enough about my books to choose those which he could sell and, of course, he would never have driven Derek's car. He always said that his Mini was as much as he could manage.' He patted his toupée with the flat of his hand. 'It would also account for the noise he made, I mean, the place was in darkness and he probably couldn't find the switches. But if he killed Derek, I suppose that he must also have killed the girl?' He broke off. 'I know that is what you were trying to tell me yesterday but, frankly, I couldn't really believe it.'

Wycliffe got out his pipe and lit it. Jarvis stared at his desk as though his thoughts were completely absorbed with the new and frightening ideas which had been presented to him.

'Did you know that Derek Robson has a criminal record?'

'No, I certainly did not! I can't believe that—'

'Two convictions for assaults on women. How did you meet him, Mr Jarvis?'

Jarvis considered. 'It must have been at least three years ago. He just walked in here one morning and spent some time looking at the books like any other customer. We got talking and it soon became obvious that he knew what he was talking about, he had a very good knowledge of French literature and he spoke the language like a native.'

'And you employed him on the strength of that?'

'Not at once. He came back several times and we grew friendly. He told me

244

that he had spent a good deal of his youth in France—at Bordeaux where his father was a wine buyer for a firm of importers in London. He went to the lycée and obtained his baccalauréat. To cut a long story short I ended up by offering him employment.'

'You did not take up references?'

'There seemed no point.'

They sat in silence for a while then Wycliffe said that he would like to take another look at the studio. They went up the two flights of stairs, past the bindery and the book-store and into the studio. Everything seemed to be as he had seen it before. Morris's picture was still on the easel and the stove filled the room with enervating warmth. He stood by the stove looking round him, he was trying to imagine the room at night with the lights on and the blue curtains drawn over the dormer windows.

At half past seven on Wednesday evening Jarvis had left Morris alone in this room.

'What was Morris doing when you left? Had he started to paint?'

Jarvis looked up from a folder of prints. 'He was working up his palette.'

Wycliffe moved over to the picture. 'The

painting seems to be finished now but it was not so then?'

'Almost but not quite, he had some work to do on it down in the bottom right, that squat building had only been blocked in.'

'And at the time you left he had not found the anonymous note?'

'If he had, he gave no sign of it.'

Presumably, at some time after Jarvis left, he had found the note in its straw coloured envelope.

'YOUR GIRL FRIEND IS A WHORE...'

What had been his reaction? Surprise? Shock? Disbelief? Finally, perhaps contempt for the writer. Anyway he had stuffed the note in the pocket of his painting jacket and gone on painting.

'How long would it have taken Morris to finish his picture?'

Jarvis was wary. 'You can never tell with Paul. He could have done what he had to do in half-an-hour, equally it might have taken him the whole evening.'

YOUR GIRL FRIEND ... FIND OUT FOR YOURSELF ... 9 STANLEY STREET. BOTTOM FLAT.

While he painted the note would never

be out of his mind. Useless to try to dismiss it. Had he finished his painting, changed his jacket, put on his overcoat and driven to Stanley Street?

It was possible—just. Perhaps he had parked in Waterloo Place and walked the rest of the way. He would have been torn between the fear of making a fool of himself and something worse. By chance he would have found Christine alone for she had cancelled her regular appointment with Harkness, the surveyor. (Why?) How would she have received him? Probably with anger, perhaps with disdainful indifference. Unforgettable and unforgivable words might have led him to—

It was possible.

And now she was lying on the floor, crumpled and limp. He would be horrified, horrified at what he had done and not less at the consequences to himself. He had read of sex crimes, the victim is always nude so he decides to strip the body. It is not easy to undress a dead girl—

'No! I don't believe it.' Wycliffe had spoken the words aloud. Everything he had heard about Morris led him to believe that, intolerably provoked, he might have killed Christine Powell but not that he could have stripped her body, lifted her on to the bed and, finally, arranged her limbs in a suggestive pose.

Jarvis was looking at him with curiosity. 'What don't you believe?'

Wycliffe ignored him. 'Did Robson own a gun?'

'A gun? Only a sort of memento of the first war. His uncle gave it to him or maybe it was his great uncle. Whoever it was had done some cloak and dagger work in Belgium and this was a Belgian officer's revolver.'

'Did he have any ammunition?'

'I don't know, dear boy, but I shouldn't think so. It was only a souvenir.'

On the way down Wycliffe stopped at the book-store. 'Have you sorted out your new consignment yet?'

'No, dear boy, I haven't had a chance to touch them. What with one thing and another...' He started to move off along the passage but Wycliffe went into the little room where books were stored on the shelves in batches of a dozen or so.

He looked them over. Most of the great names of 19th-century French literature were represented: Hugo, Dumas, Flaubert, Maupassant, Zola—Wycliffe recognized many old favourites in the unfamiliar guise of their mother tongue but he was surprised to see that most of them seemed to be in pre-war library editions and in poor condition. No first editions here. With Jarvis watching and looking increasingly concerned, Wycliffe removed books from two or three of the bundles and flicked through their pages. He even shook them by their bindings before replacing them on the shelves. As far as he could judge they were exactly what they seemed to be, second-hand books, moderately priced, popular editions of the French classics published in the years immediately before the first war. Their English counterparts would now sell on market stalls at a few pence each.

'I really don't understand what you're looking for, Mr Wycliffe.' Jarvis's tone was plaintive.

'Are these worth importing?'

'Along with more valuable works, dear boy. It would be foolish to come back with the van more than half empty.'

'But you have a sale for these?'

'Oh, yes, there is quite a demand for

them from sixth formers doing modern languages for their "A" levels.'

Wycliffe allowed himself to be piloted down the stairs and through the shop. By the time they reached the shop door Jarvis had recovered a good deal of his poise.

'You will keep me informed of any developments, dear boy? You can imagine how I feel, both those boys were like sons to me.'

Wycliffe had walked away a couple of paces when he turned back. 'Do you know if there is a ferry due in this afternoon?'

'A ferry?'

'Cross-channel'

All Jarvis's newly won composure deserted him. For a moment he seemed scarcely able to speak then he mumbled, 'I really have no idea.'

'Never mind, I can ring the docks.'

As he turned up the cobbled alley to where he had parked his car he found DC Fowler waiting for him. Fowler was a master at keeping obo, he could stand in a busy street or loiter in a deserted square without drawing attention to himself, he had the knack of looking as much part of the scene as a lamp-post.

'I saw you go in, sir, I wondered if you

had any fresh instructions for me?'

Wycliffe hesitated, he was still very unsure of his ground. 'You've got transport?'

'Parked just round the corner.'

'Car radio?'

'Yes, sir.'

'Good! It's just possible that Jarvis may come out driving the van or, perhaps, the Jag. If he does, follow him and report.'

Wycliffe continued up the slope to his car and joined the unending stream of traffic into the city. It took him twenty minutes to cover the three miles to his headquarters.

He was convinced that Robson and Jarvis had been engaged in some profitable swindle but unless it was linked with the murder of Christine Powell he did not feel immediately concerned. Privately, though with no admissible evidence, he had acquitted Paul Morris of killing the girl; but it could still have been Morris who survived the presumed struggle in the Middle Street flat and, later, went to the Old Custom House to steal a few carefully selected books which would enable him to obtain enough money to have some chance of getting away.

He climbed the stairs to his office in a mood of depression. Already he was establishing fixed patterns of behaviour in his new surroundings. When his mood was buoyant he used the lift, when he was gloomy or frustrated he laboured up the stairs. He feared that his case was 'closing down for Christmas'. Police work largely depends on information received from the public and the flow of information is stimulated by press, radio and TV. But for two days there would be no newspapers and murder does not make good Christmas broadcasting.

But there was news for him—two items.

Paul Morris's car, the blue Mini, had been found, abandoned, near Taunton. A farmer had reported the car because it was blocking the entrance to one of his fields. The farm was not far out of the town and close to the main road. The farmer was quite sure that the car had not been there the previous evening at nine o'clock.

Wycliffe consulted a map. Taunton was eighty miles away. Where had the car been since Thursday? Forty-eight hours to travel eighty miles. He put through a call to Taunton CID. They had found a suitcase in the boot containing five large illustrated books, the ignition key was in place on a ring with four other keys. The car had been brought in and was being subjected to rigorous examination. Wycliffe asked for the keys to be sent on at once.

He was led to his second piece of news through a message asking him to telephone Dr Bell, head of Forensic, an old friend.

'You're in luck, my lad! The brooch the girl was wearing—your chap couldn't find any print on it and neither could we, but one of our youngsters decided to try a new test for latents. It's supposed to be better than the old ninhydrin test on some surfaces and it depends on a reaction with urea in the sweat. Frankly, I thought he was wasting his time, the brooch is a cameo-type thing with a surface which looks like glazed porcelain. In fact it came up rather well with two quite good partial thumb prints. I've had them photographed and blown up for you.'

Wycliffe thanked him and rang off. He gave instructions for prints to be obtained from articles handled by Morris and by Robson so that they would have a basis for comparison. Soon he would have a strong pointer to the killer. But what of the car? Presumably one of the two missing men, the one whose body was not now in the mortuary, had driven it to Taunton, abandoned it and gone on from there? But why leave it down a country lane? It would have been far less conspicuous and might have passed unnoticed for days on a public car park in Taunton or anywhere else. And why leave the valuable books which were, supposedly, to be turned into money?

The Taunton police would be questioning railway officials and circulars were going out for drivers who might have picked up a hitch-hiker on the Taunton road, but Wycliffe was by no means satisfied. Could the car be a deliberate plant? If so, with what purpose? In any event somebody must have driven it to where it was found. Sheer panic might explain the whole thing if the runaway was Morris.

A tap at the door and Bellings, the assistant chief, came in. The two men fenced more or less amicably for a quarter of an hour then Bellings said, with an air of discovery, 'It's Christmas, Charles.' Which was followed a little later by what Wycliffe feared most, 'Do you know, Charles, although we have worked together for years, we have never met socially? Never! Our wives have not met.

Do you realize that?'

Wycliffe said that he did but that the case would make it impossible for him to arrange anything over Christmas. His manner of saying it was none too gracious but Bellings was not offended.

'You carry too much on your own shoulders, Charles. Delegate. Gill is a good officer, isn't he?'

'First rate.'

'Well, then.'

How could he explain that he enjoyed being on the ground, that the job would not be worth doing unless he was doing the job of a real 'jack'? Bellings was an administrator, born to sit at a desk, and he would never understand. Wycliffe mumbled something about 'getting together in the New Year' and Bellings said that he would hold him to it. 'Relax, Charles.'

As Bellings was leaving the telephone rang. It was DC Fowler who had been keeping an eye on the Old Custom House. 'I'm at the rubbish disposal plant, sir. Three quarters of an hour ago Jarvis drove out in his van as you said he might and I followed him here. He had a word with the foreman then he unloaded a number of parcels from his van and drove off. Instead of following him again I went into the works and asked the foreman not to dispose of the parcels until I had contacted you.'

'I'll be with you as soon as I can.'

He was not yet familiar with the city and he was anxious to become so. Until he knew it at least as well as any taxi-driver he would not be content. He consulted a street map and worked out a route which, at first, took him over familiar ground, down Prince's Street to the docks. Dusk was closing over the city, the street lamps were on and cars were driving with side-lights. Parents, with children trailing behind, were coming away from the market with Christmas trees that they had bought at knock-down prices. Soon Brenda, Lesley Birch and all their colleagues would be walking their beats or sitting, hopefully, in some smoky bar. 'Hullo, darling!'

He entered a maze of streets on the perimeter of the docks, rows of little brick houses. For the most part the fronts of the houses were blind and dark but occasionally there would be a rectangle of yellow light from a sitting-room that was, for once, being used. Then he was out of the maze and driving past warehouses with occasional glimpses of the water between them. The new waste disposal unit, pride of the city, had been built on a promontory of reclaimed ground, a squat complex of buildings and a chimney stack silhouetted against an angry sunset sky.

He drove into the yard and got out of his car. He was surprised at the bitter wind blowing across the estuary from the east. Fowler came out of a little brick box of an office situated at some distance from the plant. He was accompanied by the foreman, both men had their collars up and shoulders hunched against the wind.

The foreman was defensively truculent. 'I don't know what all this is about. Mr Jarvis often brings us parcels of books to burn, books which are of no use to him.'

'How often?'

The man stared out over the darkening water, he was slow moving and slow thinking. 'Three, maybe four times a year.'

'Since when?'

'Since the plant started two-and-a-half years ago.'

'Did it never occur to you to ask him why he wanted to get rid of all these books?'

The man turned his gaze on Wycliffe. 'It's no business of mine what ratepayers do, what they choose to throw away—'

'Did you ever ask him?'

'As a matter of fact, I did, just out of curiosity. He said that in order to buy a particular second-hand book he wanted he often had to buy a lot of rubbish with it.'

'I'm going to take these parcels away with me but I'll give you a receipt.'

The man shrugged. 'I suppose it's all right if you say so.'

They loaded the parcels into the two cars and Fowler and Wycliffe drove back to headquarters. There the parcels were unloaded into one of the interview rooms on the ground floor.

Wycliffe lifted one of the parcels on to the table and opened it: seven books of the kind he had seen in the attic at the Old Custom House. Fowler watched him with phlegmatic calm. He took the first book—Flaubert's *Madame Bovary,* flicked through the pages, shook it, peered down the spine then he looked at the edges of the cover boards.

'Have you got a sharp knife?'

Fowler produced a little knife with a

razor-sharp blade and Wycliffe slit the cover boards through their thickness. Nothing. He repeated the same operations on three other books but it was only when he slit the covers of the fifth, a strongly bound edition of Dumas' *The Count of Monte Cristo* that he found what he was looking for: a cavity in each of the covers, rectangular in shape and in depth about half the thickness of the covers.

Fowler said merely, 'Drugs?'

'I suppose so but empty now, of course.'

In the next four books they found another cache.

'There are about two-hundred books in this batch; if one in five of them has been treated like this it could mean a kilo of heroin or whatever the stuff is... You'd better see if Inspector Webb is in the building.'

Inspector Webb was head of the drugs squad.

Fowler went across the passage to a room with a telephone and a few minutes later Webb arrived. His work was a crusade. Given any lead he was unremitting in his efforts to follow it to a conclusion and he spared neither himself nor his men. He hated drugs as though their very chemical substance had been endowed with a terrible malignancy. Perhaps he had seen too much of the misery caused by their misuse to remain objective. He was several years younger than Wycliffe and, of course, junior in rank, but his attitude was brusque, almost rude, as though by his very discovery Wycliffe had incurred a moral responsibility.

Back in his office Wycliffe sent for Jimmy Gill and put him in charge of the operation that would have to be mounted at the Old Custom House. 'I'll leave it to you, Jimmy, to work with Webb.'

Was this what the case was all about? Perhaps. But his interest still centred on the fact that a girl and a man had died violent deaths. Not for the first time he reflected that people have a choice whether or not they take the first steps towards drug addiction, but very few people elect to be maimed or murdered. Society, almost morbid in its anxiety to protect us against ourselves, is less concerned in protecting us against the predations of others.

Wycliffe decided to spend as much of Christmas day as possible at home but the mass of paper work on his desk weighed on his conscience. He rang for WPC Saxton and she came in, as always, with her notebook at the ready. 'I'm working on for a while to clear up some of this, perhaps you would ask them to send up a tray from the canteen?'

His tray arrived, tea with two hot mince-pies all runny with fresh cream. He offered one to WPC Saxton and watched her eat it without once having to lick her fingers. How was it done?

He worked steadily while the lights in the offices throughout the building went out, one by one, and the traffic along the highroad dwindled to an occasional car. At half past eight Gill came in, looking tired.

'Well, sir, your friend Jarvis coughed.'

Wycliffe did not deny the soft impeachment. He had to admit that he felt sorry for Jarvis now though he had had little but contempt for him before. It had not taken Gill long to get his story, Jarvis had seemed anxious to unburden himself once confronted. He had refused a lawyer. For years Jarvis had made his trips to France conducting an honest business then, along came Robson with a sound knowledge of books, fluent in French and eminently plausible. An opportunist, he had wormed his way into Jarvis's life and business so that, before long, it was he who made the routine trips across the channel and soon book buying was little more than a cover for drug trafficking. Jarvis said that he did not know the details but Robson had told him that the drug was heroin, prepared from opium brought into Marseilles. Make-shift laboratories, set up in any disused building, flitted ahead of police raids always, apparently, forewarned.

'He doesn't seem a bad little man,' Gill said, 'just weak, but it will go hard with him now.'

The dear boy approach was unlikely to do him much good with prosecuting counsel or with the judge. Judges don't like queers and they have a strong prejudice against drug pedlars.

Despite the most thorough search Webb had failed to find any heroin and Jarvis claimed that he had no idea where Robson had taken it after removing it from the books.

Wycliffe said, 'I wish I knew why Jarvis tried to dispose of the books. He would have been in a much stronger position if he had left them in his store.'

'But you expected him to, you told Fowler—'

'I didn't *expect* him to, I merely gave him the opportunity and he took it.'

'Well?'

'He's not stupid.' Wycliffe looked up at the clock. 'It's Christmas Eve, Jimmy, you should be at home with your youngsters.'

Gill yawned and stood up. 'Perhaps you're right. Merry Christmas.'

Wycliffe returned to the papers on his desk but found it impossible to concentrate. At half past nine he gave up. As he left the building through the duty room a single officer wished him 'Good night.'

He drove home once more through empty streets under the neon and tinsel stars. Few of the shops had left their lights on. For them it was over, shelves and stockrooms had been stripped, night-safes were bulging and managers were deciding whether they were 'up' or 'down' on last year and calculating their commissions. Now the cash registers in the pubs were making their own kind of music and soon it would be the turn of the angels.

CHAPTER TEN

Eleven o'clock on Christmas morning. Wycliffe was standing at the living-room window, looking out over the narrows. Cold and brittle sunshine but brilliant. Helen's embryo trees and shrubs looked forlorn. For once the narrows were deserted, not a craft in sight, only gulls wheeling and swooping, presumably over a school of fish. Presents had been exchanged. Wycliffe was wearing his new finely knitted, lambswool cardigan and his fleece-lined slippers. David was in the bathroom trying out his new electric shaver, Helen was in the kitchen preparing the meal. Ruth's new transistor sounded faintly from her bedroom upstairs. She came into the living-room still in her dressing-gown, her blonde hair held back by a slide, like a little girl's. She smiled at him, an enigmatic smile, a young woman's smile; he hadn't a clue what she was thinking or what she ever thought. She glided round the house wrapped in herself and sometimes she irritated him, but Helen seemed not to mind. 'It's her age, she'll get over it.'

The day stretched ahead like an expanse of featureless desert. A surfeit of food, emasculated TV, lame efforts at conviviality. The feast of the family. They would end by reading in their separate corners. He left the window and walked through to the kitchen.

The turkey was in the oven, the pudding simmering on the hotplate.

'Bored?'

'I wondered if I could help.'

'You can wash up, if you like, but put your apron on.'

He had a butcher's apron, blue with horizontal, white stripes of which he was secretly proud.

He did not wash up, instead he prowled about the house. He was waiting, but for what? He had no idea himself.

Morris did not kill Christine Powell. He had convinced himself of that. In any case there had been a flaw in his imaginative reconstruction which told in Morris's favour. Robson had gone into the studio at twenty minutes to eight and found Morris there, painting. '...working on that city centre thing.' Well, the painting was now finished and Morris's brushes and palette had been cleaned and put away. If Christine Powell had been killed between half past eight and nine, as Franks said, then Morris had to find the note, finish his picture, clean his brushes and palette and get to Stanley Street all in under the hour. Unlikely from any point of view.

His perambulations brought him back to the kitchen. 'What about a sherry?'

'Too early.'

'It's Christmas.'

'All right, but only a small one for me.'

He poured a small one for his wife, a larger one for himself and took his drink into the living-room. He stood, once more, staring out of the window, sipping his drink from time to time. Ruth was sitting in an armchair turning the pages of the *Radio Times*.

If not Morris then Robson...

'I'd never realized there was so much money in second-hand books.' Christine Powell speaking. If she had discovered where the money really came from the smallest indiscretion might have cost her her life. Perhaps it had.

Back to Wednesday evening at the Old Custom House. Jarvis had gone out, Morris was in the studio working on his painting. Robson was in his room, probably listening to records. He went to the studio, ostensibly to collect a pen he had left there, actually to satisfy himself that Morris had settled down to work. Robson could have put on Morris's overcoat. Wycliffe had noticed an old-fashioned hall-stand at the bottom of the stairs. Morris probably hung his coat there as he came in. And he probably left his car keys in the pocket of his overcoat. Christine Powell had cancelled Harkness's appointment—because she knew that Robson was coming? In which case the thing had been planned in advance. But there was a snag, the note which he had found in the pocket of Morris's painting jacket. Unless the note was a coincidence but Wycliffe did not like coincidences. If Robson was setting Morris up it would have been easy and prudent to plant such a note *after* the crime.

'Telephone! It's for you.'

He had scarcely heard the telephone ringing and Ruth had answered it. He took the receiver from her.

'Wycliffe.'

It was Scales. 'You left word that you were to be kept informed, sir. I've compared the blow-ups of the prints on the dead girl's brooch with those of Robson and Morris. There's no doubt at all that they match Robson's. I've found fourteen points of correspondence without difficulty.

'So all we've got to do now is find him.'

'Unless we've already got him, sir.'

That, of course, was the problem, they still did not know whether it was Robson or Morris whose body lay in the mortuary. Dr Franks had succeeded in getting a blood grouping—A, Rhesus positive—but they had been quite unable to find out the groups to which either man belonged.

The finding of Morris's car worried Wycliffe, the evidence of flight was unconvincing. Who, in his right mind, would abandon a road-worthy car and leave in it a large part of his capital, in the middle of the night, in the middle of nowhere? Yet the car had been driven down the farm lane and abandoned by somebody.

And Jarvis had virtually given himself up—why? It could have been panic but

Wycliffe did not think so. Once he had seen that the police were suspicious he had almost deliberately laid himself open to arrest.

Wycliffe went to the telephone again and dialled his headquarters. He was put through to the duty officer. 'Has Mr Jarvis gone back to his shop?'

'No, sir, he's still in the cells. He refused bail.'

'On what grounds?'

'He wouldn't give a reason, sir; he just said that he preferred to remain in custody.'

There must be a very good reason why a man as set in his habits as Jarvis would elect to stay in a police cell rather than return to his own home. Wycliffe thought that he could guess that reason.

'I'm coming in to talk to him, have him brought up to my office in half an hour. Is Sergeant Scales still in CID?'

'I don't think so, sir, but DC Dixon was there a few minutes ago.'

'If he's still there tell him to join me in my office.'

Wycliffe dropped the receiver and went into the kitchen. His wife was basting the turkey and Ruth was staring out of the window though there was nothing to be seen but the backyard. 'I'm sorry, dear, but I have to go out.'

'For long?'

'Very likely.'

Helen looked ruefully at the turkey. 'I could hold the meal back until this evening.'

'Just save me a bit.' He kissed her on the ear. Ruth had turned away from the window and was looking at him with mild incredulity.

'You should join a union!'

He drove through the city, there were few people about and those few looked out of place, walking aimlessly. He felt guilty because he had escaped. On the CID floor he found Jarvis seated in the waiting room with Dixon. Javis looked older, his cavalry twill hung loosely from his shoulders as though he had shrunk.

'Mr Jarvis...' Wycliffe ushered him into his office and signalled to Dixon to remain outside. He waved Jarvis to a chair and the bookseller sat blinking in the strong light from the big window.

Jarvis said, vaguely, 'It's Christmas, isn't it?'

'So you refused bail?'

Jarvis blinked and nodded. 'I don't want bail.'

'Any particular reason?'

Jarvis shook his head but did not reply.

'You don't have to answer my questions but there seems no reason for you to make things more unpleasant for yourself than they need to be. Tomorrow you will be remanded and your trial may be weeks ahead. If there was an application for bail the police would not object.'

'No.' Emphatic.

'Why not?'

Again a shake of the head.

'Perhaps you feel safer in custody?'

Jarvis looked at him sharply, 'I don't know what you mean.' His hands rested in his lap, the fingers twitching nervously.

'I think you do.' Wycliffe was watching him with an unwavering stare that was neither antagonistic, nor compassionate. He was beginning to sense the relationship which had grown up between Jarvis and his assistant, it had the smell of fear. To begin with Robson could have been the model employee, intelligent, informed, anxious to please. Jarvis was gently encouraged to loose the reins, to hand over. He was getting old and increasingly aware of his loneliness. Robson took over the buying, the trips to France, and soon there was more money about, more for him to spend on his precious books. At first he did not enquire too closely and by the time he did things had gone too far. Step by step he had been enticed like a pigeon following a trail of scattered grain.

'You have lived with this man on your back for long enough. When did you last have any say in the running of your business or, for that matter, in the running of your life?'

Jarvis shook his head.

'Where is he now?'

'I don't know.'

'But he did come back on Thursday night after the fire?'

'Yes.' In a small voice.

Wycliffe spread his hands in a gesture which invited more.

'He came back after I had gone to bed, that much of what I told you was true. He came into my room...'

'And?'

'He just stood inside the door and said, "You're talking to a dead man, you don't get the chance very often so make the most of it."'

'Did he tell you what had happened?'

'Not a word. He just told me what I was to say to the police if they started asking questions.'

'And what was that?'

Jarvis flushed. 'Exactly what I told you. I was to lead you to believe without actually saying so that it was Morris who came back after the fire. Then he said, "You'll be missing a few of your books in the morning, Morris will need some fluid assets and I'm sure you won't begrudge him." He stood there so...so arrogant, so pleased with himself, *knowing* that I would do what he wanted... If I could have killed him at that moment.'

'Did you see him in the morning?'

'I haven't seen him since.'

'But you don't think he's far away?'

It was pathetic. Jarvis's lips trembled and he shook his head but no words came. In the end he said, 'Is that all?'

'Unless there is something I can do for you?'

'No, nothing.'

'Something to read?'

A very faint smile. 'The sergeant has left me some thrillers.'

Wycliffe called Dixon in. As Jarvis

reached the door he looked back, as though seeing the room for the first time. 'It's odd isn't it?'

'What is?'

'I don't know, you and me...'

When he was alone Wycliffe spoke to the officer in charge of crime cars. He gave instructions for two cars to be stationed near the Old Custom House, one in the square and the other in Bear Street but they were not to take up their positions for forty-five minutes.

Dixon came back looking puzzled. 'Is he all right in the head, sir?'

'Why do you ask?'

'He told me to remind you about the gun.'

Wycliffe collected Jarvis's keys from the duty desk and they drove to his customary parking place at the top of the alley leading to the harbour. There was no unending stream of traffic today, not a car in sight, even the parking meters were hooded.

'Do you know this district, Dixon?'

'Not well, sir, I've been out fishing from the harbour once or twice.'

The reached the harbour; only the gulls mincing along the edge of the wharf, eyeing the water for any scrap of food.

The shops had their blinds down. Despite the sunshine it was cold, a cutting wind off the water, and they were glad of their overcoats.

Dixon was mystified and fascinated. He had had his part in the case but he knew little or nothing of its ramifications. He had heard of the drugs raid on the Old Custom House but he had only the haziest notion of how it was linked with the fire in Middle Street and the murder of Christine Powell.

Wycliffe unlocked the shop door and they entered its musty atmosphere. Already the place seemed cold and untenanted. Dixon followed him through the rows of books, through the passage where Jarvis exhibited his pictures, to the back door. Wycliffe fumbled for the right key, found it, and they were out in the sunshine once more, the dappled sunshine which filtered through the great spreading canopy of the cedar.

Wycliffe had not been in the courtyard before and young Dixon did not know of its existence. The weedy cobbles and the cedar backed by weathered stonework gave the place a sense of timelessness, of unreality, but reality intruded from a radio in one of the Bear Street houses.

Robson's Jaguar was still parked beyond the cedar but the black van was in one of several open sheds which occupied the far side of the courtyard. At the Bear Street end there were double doors and next to them a house with a yard railed off from the courtyard by a rotting fence.

Wycliffe said, 'This is where the girl in the snaps you found lives, the freckled girl. It's a café round the front.'

As they reached the fence the girl herself opened the back door and came out into the yard with a bowl of vegetable peelings. She saw them and recognized Wycliffe.

'You! What do you want?'

'Is your father in?'

'He's over to the pub and you'll not see him till closing time.'

There was a crude gate in the fence and Wycliffe passed through followed by Dixon. She eyed them with evident misgiving.

'I suppose you'd better come in.'

The kitchen was not large considering that it must cater for the restaurant trade: a gas range, a hot closet, a freezer, double sinks and draining boards round the walls and a large, deal table in the middle. There was an appetizing smell of stew coming from a pot on the cooker.

'No turkey?'

She grinned. 'We get tired of all that; when the café is closed we go for a good stew.'

'You get on well with your father?'

She looked surprised. 'He's all right when he can keep off the drink.'

'Do you tell him everything?'

'I don't know what you're talking about.'

'Do you enjoy night-driving?'

She had her back to him so that he could not see her expression but her manner was derisive. 'What is this, some sort of game?'

'What did you do on Friday night, the night before last?'

She was putting cloves of garlic in a press and she did not answer.

'What time did you leave? Midnight? About then, I think. Say, two and a half hours driving and you would arrive at about half past two in the morning. You left the car in a lane which you thought was rarely used then you had to walk to the station. There was a train at three-thirty-five which got you here at five-thirty. All you had to do was walk home; in bed by six and father none the wiser. A good night's work.'

She had moved over to the range and was scraping crushed garlic into the stew. 'I can't stop you from talking, can I?'

'How many people were there taking tickets at Taunton Station when you took yours? Not many. The clerk will remember you. You must have travelled down in a compartment with other people, a girl, travelling alone, is noticed. If we put your picture on TV we should soon be hearing from them.'

There was silence broken only by the ticking of the kitchen clock and the gentle, irregular bubbling of the stew. Dixon was mesmerized, unable to guess where it was all leading. In the end she said, 'All right! I helped him get away, make what you can of it.'

So far Wycliffe's manner had been friendly, relaxed and affable. Suddenly he became peremptory. 'Look at me! You should be quite clear about one thing in your own interest; I know that Paul Morris is dead and it is Robson you are shielding.'

His sudden change of tactics had startled her for a moment, she looked at him with frightened eyes but soon recovered her poise. 'All right, it was Derek I helped to get away.'

Wycliffe relaxed again. 'But you helped nobody to get away, you made the trip alone. Robson is still—'

She was too quick for him, he had fully expected that she would begin by a denial but instead she flew out of the kitchen and almost before he realized what was happening he could hear her racing up the stairs.

'You stay here!' To Dixon.

The stairs led off a small, dark hall between the kitchen and the restaurant. They led to a landing and passage with three or four doors off but the girl had continued up a second flight, narrower and steeper, presumably to an attic or attics. By the time Wycliffe had reached the first landing the girl was at the top of the second flight. He heard a door open then slam and not another sound.

He was angry with himself, what had happened he had foreseen as a possibility yet he had allowed it to happen. In all probability Robson would use the girl as a hostage and there would be a Christmas circus with a police siege of the house with people bleating through loud hailers, a gala day for the press and TV. Unless he could be talked out of it. Wycliffe thought it worth trying. He climbed the remaining stairs at a more leisurely pace.

At the top there was a short passage lit by a skylight with two doors off. The first was open into an empty room with light coming from a dusty, cob-webbed dormer window. The second door was shut.

Wycliffe knew that he was taking a silly risk with a man who delighted in violence but he felt surprisingly calm. It was afterwards, perhaps days later, that he would feel the cold shivers down his spine. He opened the second door and stood in the doorway; there was no immediate threat to him. The girl and Robson were sitting side by side on a camp bed. The man had his hand over her mouth and nostrils, crumpling her cheeks in a cruel grip; in his other hand he held the gun.

Wycliffe showed neither surprise or concern. 'There's no point in stifling her, what possible difference can it make if she screams?'

Robson hesitated for a moment then, with a shrug, released his hold.

Wycliffe said, 'I've come to take you in for questioning.'

'You're a cool bastard, I'll say that for you.'

The girl was fingering her jaw but she showed no disposition to scream.

Wycliffe was trying to judge the temper of the man; his manner was self-confident, cocky. As long as he stayed that way there was little risk of him resorting to violence. 'If you use that gun you will be putting yourself away for a long time.'

'I'm not counting on using it if you and your lot behave. I've got it all worked out. All you have to do is to have my car brought round the front with a full tank. Babs and I will go down and drive off together. No trouble to anybody.' He looked at Wycliffe with a crooked grin.

'That sounds reasonable.'

'I'm glad you think so. Just one other thing—no tail. At the first sign of a copper—' He jerked the gun. 'I want sixteen hours, after that you can unleash your bloodhounds.'

'You are taking this young lady as a hostage?'

'If you like to call it that.'

'What do you think about it?' Wycliffe addressed the girl.

'I'll go with him, it will be all right if you do as he says.'

Robson nodded. 'She's a sensible girl.'

Wycliffe looked at him with a quizzical expression. 'Do you read thrillers?'

'What's that got to do with it?'

'You seem anxious to dramatize your situation—to make it sound more desperate than it appears.'

Robson was not smiling now, he was wary, obviously puzzled. 'What are you after, copper? What exactly do you want me for?'

'For questioning in connection with the deaths of Christine Powell and Paul Morris.'

'There you are, then! That's desperate enough for my money.'

'Did you murder either of these people?'

'No, but with my record—'

Wycliffe cut in:'I think you should know that the pathologist is satisfied that Morris died in a struggle.'

'Is that on the level?'

'It is, and there's something else: a man has come forward who says he saw Paul Morris leaving the house in Stanley Street shortly after the time at which we believe Christine Powell was murdered.'

Wycliffe salved his conscience with the thought that he was telling the truth, if not the whole truth.

The girl became animated: 'I told you, Derek!...'

Robson snapped: 'You shut up!' He turned back to Wycliffe. 'So why do you want me?'

'Because, for whatever reason and in whatever circumstances, it was you who killed Morris. You may still face a lesser charge than murder on that account.'

So far there had been no mention of drugs and Wycliffe counted on the likelihood that Robson did not know that his racket had been discovered. Robson's next question confirmed this: 'What's happened to Jarvis? Babs, here, says he isn't at the shop.'

Wycliffe was casually matter-of-fact: 'He was detained and questioned on suspicion of aiding your escape.'

Robson laughed. 'That's damned funny! Don't you think that's funny, Babs?'

The girl nodded without conviction. Robson sobered, 'I need time to think about this.'

Wycliffe relaxed. For the first time he had a chance to look round the little room. Apart from the camp-bed there was a chair and a card-table with a green baize top. An old fashioned oil-heater with a fretted iron top stood near the bed and gave the room a moist, stuffy warmth. There were newspapers on the floor by the bed and an empty mug. Robson wore the black slacks and sweater he had worn when Wycliffe first met him, but now they were covered with fluff from the bedding and he had two or three days' growth of beard. The girl, apparently passive, was sitting with her hands in her lap.

'Does your father know about your guest?'

She shook her head. 'He's not a man who takes a big interest in what goes on around him unless it's somebody opening a bottle.'

Robson said: 'I'd be ready to make a deal if—'

'No deals!'

Wycliffe saw his jaw muscles tighten along with his grip on the gun. 'You're not in a position to argue, copper.'

Wycliffe spoke quietly. 'Get this into your head: you can drive off with your girl friend, you can have your sixteen hours and much good will it do you. You'll be caught and there'll be an additional crop of charges.' He sounded indifferent, almost bored.

The girl looked from him to her companion and back again; she seemed about to speak but changed her mind.

Robson said: 'You're bloody sure of yourself.'

'Because these hostage tricks are for cocky teenagers and half-wits. They never work.'

There was minor commotion in the street below. A man's voice, thick with drink, and somebody banging on the door of the café.

'That will be father.'

Wycliffe said, 'You'd better go down and let him in.'

She looked at Robson and after a moment of hesitation he nodded. Wycliffe stepped aside to let her pass and when he heard her footsteps on the stairs he heaved a great sigh of relief. 'If you shoot me they'll give you thirty years straight off so you'd better give me that before it goes off.'

CHAPTER ELEVEN

'I suppose that, in a way, I was responsible for Christine's death.' Robson was relaxed, almost genial, pleased with himself.

Wycliffe sat at his desk. A stenographer with his pad was placed behind Robson; Jimmy Gill stood by the window. Gill and the stenographer had had their Christmas dinners but Wycliffe and Robson had made do with stale sandwiches and coffee from an understaffed canteen.

Outside, contrary to the forecast, the sky was leaden with snow clouds and at any moment the first fall of the winter would begin.

'You wish to make a statement?'

'That was the idea.'

Wycliffe was subdued, slow and deliberate. 'Very well; you have been cautioned but not yet charged with any offence.' He glanced up at the clock set in the wooden panelling of his office. 'This interview begins at three-twenty.'

Robson spoke without pause or interruption for several minutes. He began confidently and only faltered when he searched for the word which best expressed his meaning. He had written the anonymous note to Paul Morris as a joke but the joke had gone sour. He had never supposed for a moment that it would result in more than an amusing confrontation which he would hear about from Christine later.

'I swear that was how it was.'

He said that he had left the note on Morris's painting table and that he had looked in later to see what had happened. The note had gone. Morris made no reference to it but a few minutes later, after returning to his room, Robson heard him drive off in his Mini.

'You can imagine how I felt next morning when I heard about Christine...'

He adopted a tragic expression and turned to Wycliffe for some sign of understanding but Wycliffe was staring at him, his features a blank. Gill was looking out of the window where the scene was like a steel engraving.

'There was nothing I could do. Nothing!'

Robson said that he had spent Thursday in the shop and that towards evening there had been a telephone call from Morris.

'He was like a madman. He insisted on meeting me at the Middle Street flat... All right! I'd been there a few times with Chris. The appointment, if that's what you could call it, was for nine o'clock. I walked there because I didn't want my car to be seen around if there was trouble.'

He looked at Wycliffe. 'You can see I'm putting my cards on the table. Anyway, Morris's Mini was parked in a loading bay behind one of the stores and I went up the steps to the flat.

'The place was in darkness and when I rang the bell there was no answer but I tried the door and it was unlocked.'

Wycliffe reflected that it was an hour later that he had stood at the top of the iron steps, ringing the doorbell. He had not had the temerity or the initiative to try the door.

Robson went on: 'I went into the kitchen, using my pocket torch as I didn't want to draw attention by switching on lights.' He looked at Wycliffe and spoke with greater deliberation: 'I had with me an old service revolver which belonged to an uncle of mine. Of course I had no intention of using it but if you'd heard Morris on the phone...'

Wycliffe's expression did not change.

'I called out but nobody answered. I must admit that I was more than a bit scared and by the time I reached the passage I had the torch in one hand and the gun in the other. In the passage there was a little light coming from the big front-room, the door of which was partly open. The light was dim and flickering as though somebody was in there with a candle. I called out but there was still no response. I pushed open the door and went in.'

Robson paused to run his hand through his thick, black hair. 'I could scarcely believe my eyes. At each end of the room there was a bucket with a lighted candle somehow floating in it and, over the bucket, somebody had constructed a crazy pyramid of furniture, paper and linen. It went through my mind that it must be part of some sort of ceremony like witchcraft or something, then it dawned on me.

'I went towards one of the things, actually the one on my right. There is an alcove at that end of the room—or there was—and as I drew level with it something made me duck. I'll never know what made me do it but if I hadn't it really would have been me you found in the ashes.' He looked up with the faintest trace of a smile. 'Morris had been standing in the alcove, waiting for me with a heavy brass thing like a pestle which Christine used as a doorstop.

'Of course, he missed me and I was in with a chance. The gun went off almost immediately when I wasn't even thinking of using it but the shot couldn't have touched him for he fought like a madman. I'd never have believed he had it in him. He was trying to get at the gun, forcing my arm down, then it happened, another shot and he went limp and just slid to the ground.' He paused. 'I was petrified!'

Robson shifted in his chair so that the castors screeched, glanced behind him, perhaps to see if the stenographer was still there, then he ran his finger round inside the collar of his sweater. 'God! It's hot in here.' No one else moved or spoke and after a brief interval he continued with his story.

For a while, he said, he had just stood there, then, as he recovered from the shock, he realized that he would almost certainly be at the receiving end of a murder charge. 'With my record!' He seemed anxious to make sure that his record was not overlooked.

'I decided to let the candles burn. I knew it was wrong but I thought it would give me a better chance and it couldn't hurt him. Then I remembered something which Christine had once pointed out, Morris and I were exactly the same height, I carried a bit more weight but...'

He looked at the carpet as though he had come to a part of his story which he found difficult. 'To cut it short, I took off my identity disc and, after making sure he didn't wear one, I put mine round his neck.' He shrugged. 'I did it on the spur of the moment.'

Robson stopped speaking and there was complete silence. The stenographer cleared his throat as though he found the silence embarrassing. From his place by the window Gill could see myriads of snow flakes scurrying down to settle on the grass and the rockeries below but the high-road was still black and shining under the street lamps.

'Is that your statement, Mr Robson?'

Robson looked mildly surprised. 'Yes.'

'Are you willing to answer one or two questions?'

A smile. 'That's what I'm here for.'

The internal telephone on Wycliffe's desk bleeped and he answered it. 'Wycliffe... Yes... No, I'll come out.' He replaced the receiver and stood up. 'Excuse me.'

He was gone for two or three minutes but the three men remaining in the room scarcely moved. Every half-minute the big hand of the wall-clock jerked forward with a little click dictated by a 'master' somewhere in the building. Another of Wycliffe's pet hates, he liked a clock he could wind and keep three minutes fast.

When he came back he resumed his former place and took up where he had left off.

'You seem to have left something out of your statement, Mr Robson. You say that you exchanged identities with the dead man, or hoped to do so, by putting your identity disc round his neck, what else did you do?'

Robson's gaze returned to the carpet. 'I'm not proud of that.'

Gill spoke for the first time. 'You took the brass pestle and delivered a smashing blow to Morris' upper jaw. Why did you do that?'

'It occurred to me that his teeth would have...well, given me away. He had all his teeth while I have a small plate in front where I lost four teeth in a rough house.'

'And then—after you delivered the blow, did you do anything else? Did you, for example, look round the rest of the flat?'

It was some time before he answered then he said, 'I looked round briefly, I don't know why.'

Wycliffe's gaze was unwavering. 'Did you find any more candles in buckets?'

'There was another in the bedroom.'

'Lit?'

'Like the others.'

'Now, Mr Robson, perhaps you will tell me what you did after you left the flat. If you want to make a full statement it will have to cover the time until your arrest this morning.'

Robson nodded. He spent some time in thought then he went on with his story. He had driven back to the Old Custom House in Morris's car having taken the keys from the body.

'You locked the flat?'

Hesitation. 'Yes, I did, I don't know why.'

'The key?'

'It was on Morris's bunch.'

'Go on.'

He had put Morris's car in a shed in Bear Street where the freckled girl kept her own Mini and, with the girl's help he had established himself in the attic. He worked on the principle that the best place to hide was under the very noses of the searchers. If he had been content to leave it at that for the time being his chances might have been better but he had tried to be too clever. Morris's car had to be found at some safe distance and he had sent the freckled girl to ditch it in some place where it would be found, but, preferably, not at once.

All through his statement which had taken almost an hour Robson had spoken in a subdued voice and a controlled manner, striving to appear not only co-operative but remorseful for his admitted part in the events he described. Now that the ordeal seemed to be over his cockiness and self-complacency returned. Almost one could hear him say, 'Make something of that, copper.'

Wycliffe got out his pipe, filled it and lit it. Only when it was drawing nicely did he speak and the interval was long enough for Robson to begin to fidget. 'As far as I can judge, you seem to have told very few unnecessary lies. That is an achievement;

most criminals cannot resist the temptation to embroider.'

Robson's expression became wooden. 'I don't understand...'

'There are two facts which your statement does not explain. When you were brought here your fingerprints were taken as a matter of routine. An expert from Forensic has compared them with a photograph of latent prints developed from the brooch Christine Powell was wearing when she died. I understand that there are more than enough points of similarity to connect you with the killing.' Wycliffe held up his hand. 'The witness who at first said that he had seen Morris leaving the Stanley Street flat turned out to be unreliable. He could, of course, be called for the defence but I doubt if they will use him.'

Robson exercised great self-control. He said, merely, 'There must be some mistake.'

Wycliffe ignored him. 'I said that there were two facts. After you were arrested this morning I arranged for officers of the drugs squad to search the premises where you were hiding. I heard just now that they have recovered approximately a kilogramme of a substance which appears to be heroin. I have evidence that heroin has been smuggled into this country by you in consignments of books.'

Robson's lips moved but he did not trust himself to speak.

'These facts will involve you in fresh charges so it is my duty to caution you afresh.' Wycliffe's voice and manner were calm, indifferent, almost disdainful.

By seven o'clock on Christmas evening Robson had completed a second statement and the CID floor was a blaze of light with someone in occupation of almost every room. Repercussions were beginning to be felt in London and several provincial towns which were regularly visited by Robson. Messages had gone out to Marseilles, Toulon, Béziers and Lyons which would rouse a good many policemen from their Christmas lethargy. A kilo of heroin is a substantial haul but it was the implication that similar amounts had travelled by a regular route which put officials on their mettle.

For Wycliffe it was the least important aspect of his case, a side-issue. What mattered to him was that a violent man would be restrained from further violence for a long time to come.

In making his second statement Robson's whole attitude seemed to have changed, he was like a different person, bombastic, truculent. Now that he realized that nothing could save him from a life sentence, that the very word mitigation was a sour joke in the context of his case, he seemed determined to get what satisfaction he could from his situation by making a parade of his guilt. Even his voice and his manner of speech had changed. So far he had been articulate, even cultured, now his words came in bursts, disjointed phrases often difficult to link together, interspersed with invective against almost anyone he happened to mention.

His real motive for killing Christine Powell remained uncertain. He said that she had started to ask awkward questions about the second-hand rubbish he took the trouble to import; then, one evening, by an unlucky chance, she had caught him in the act of removing heroin from the covers of a book.

'So you killed her to keep her quiet?'

A complacent smile. 'Wrong again, copper. I killed her because she tried to screw me like she screwed the stupid bastards in Stanley Street.'

'Blackmail?'

He nodded. 'Of a sort. The chick had really fallen for me and she wanted me to marry her to shut her mouth.'

For some reason which he could not quite analyse, Wycliffe hoped that this was a lie.

Whatever his motive Robson had told the girl to expect him at a time when he knew that Paul Morris would be alone in the studio at the Old Custom House. He had worn Morris's overcoat and he had driven the blue Mini.

The note—'YOUR GIRL FRIEND IS A WHORE...' had been part of his scheme to incriminate Morris and he had placed it in the painting jacket after the crime. Morris had never set eyes on it.

Real trouble began for Robson late on Thursday afternoon when Morris telephoned in a highly excited state. He accused Robson outright and demanded to talk to him under threat of going to the police.

'Christ! he scared me, I couldn't make out his angle then. I mean, if he had the dirt on me, why didn't he sing straight? But I couldn't risk calling his bluff, he always was an unpredictable sod.'

He stuck to his story that it was Morris who had insisted on meeting in the Middle Street flat and that it was Morris who had rigged the fire. 'You think that I would have put a foot in there with the cops likely to bust in at any minute? But I had no option.' He paused. 'It was like I said, he'd fixed to burn the place down and me with it. He was a bloody madman, not fit to be loose. And all for a bloody tart!'

It was as far as they got but it was far enough. To Wycliffe it made a kind of sense, it completed a pattern. Paul Morris had decided there was nothing left for him to live for; he had tried Robson, found him guilty, and decided that they should go together. But like most of the really important things in his life it had gone wrong.

At a little after nine o'clock Wycliffe drove home over roads that were crisp with newly fallen snow. The moon had risen and the sky was clear. The navigation lights in the estuary twinkled like stars. Helen and the twins were playing Canasta but they stopped to feed him with cold turkey and salad washed down with his favourite hock.

As he ate he was thinking; not of Robson or Jarvis; not of the dead girl, nor of the ill-starred Morris; he had in his mind an image of the little upstair flat at 9 Stanley Street, and of Brenda, the prostitute, with her feet up, watching the television.

This Large Print Book for the Partially sighted, who cannot read normal print, is published under the auspices of

THE ULVERSCROFT FOUNDATION

THE ULVERSCROFT FOUNDATION

. . . we hope that you have enjoyed this Large Print Book. Please think for a moment about those people who have worse eyesight problems than you . . . and are unable to even read or enjoy Large Print, without great difficulty.

You can help them by sending a donation, large or small to:

**The Ulverscroft Foundation,
1, The Green, Bradgate Road,
Anstey, Leicestershire, LE7 7FU,
England.**
or request a copy of our brochure for more details.

The Foundation will use all your help to assist those people who are handicapped by various sight problems and need special attention.

Thank you very much for your help.